Punchers Creek

Rube Cassidy rode from Cedar Springs with a small herd and a big pack of trouble.

Wild Bird cattle ranch had laid untended and overgrown for ten years waiting for its lawful owner to return. But the land's plentiful water supply and fertile soil had not gone unnoticed by the covetous eyes of sheep men Greasy Quorrel and Clete Winder.

And when Etta Hark becomes a hostage in their plan to overrun Wild Bird, the door is open at last for Rube to wreak the long-harboured retribution of a man who has been crossed once too often.

By the same author

Ironhead
The Landbreakers
The Frightened Valley
Borderline
Death Song
Shot Gold

Punchers Creek

ABE DANCER

A Black Horse Western

ROBERT HALE · LONDON

ISBN 0 7090 7678 9

Robert Hale Limited
Clerkenwell House
Clerkenwell Green
London EC1R 0HT

Typeset by
Derek Doyle & Associates, Shaw Heath.
Printed and bound in Great Britain by
Antony Rowe Limited, Wiltshire

1

COOLIDGE

Outside of the Running Steer Saloon, several horses bore the Red Iron brand. Others were Snakehead or Lone Tree. It was a rowdy cattlemen's house, and Ruben Cassidy decided to walk his roan mare on, hitch it further along the street.

There were fewer customers in Cuffy Deke's. Two men were playing cards, and drinking at a table, and three were standing near one end of the bar. Rube walked towards them, stopped alongside a cloth-covered platter. The bartender saw him and came over. He took out a handful of salt-beans, lifted a bottle and glass on to the mahogany. Rube nodded, turned half-interested to the testy exchange ahead of him.

Louis Hark, editor of the *Coolidge Broadcast* was angry, but apparently not at his companions. It was plain, they'd all been arguing for some time, and the newspaper man was in a fair steam.

'I'm tellin' you, this range is goin' to be covered with blood before long,' he insisted.

'There's nothin' in the county ordinance that covers sabre-rattlin',' one of the other men said. It was only when the man picked up his whiskey glass, that Rube saw the silver star of a county sheriff, pinned to the lapel of his coat.

'I can only do somethin' when there's actual violence, an' so far, there ain't been none,' Sheriff Digby Wonnok continued.

'For Chris'sakes, Sheriff, both factions are gatherin'. It's some sort o' fool that can't see there's another war brewin'. An' most likely, right here in town.' Hark aired his fearful annoyance.

'You're boilin' over,' Wonnok said tolerantly. 'An' the town's got itself an able marshal in Dub, here. Anyways, what makes you think the sheepmen are goin' to move in? All the land around here's owned an' occupied. Specially along Ten Mile Creek. They try grabbin' *that*, an' they'll have a goddamn US marshal on top of 'em.'

Rube thumb-flicked a bean to his mouth, gave the barman another nod and took a refill.

'For myself, I don't give a damn, for either side.' The sheriff was pursuing his take on the situation. 'My concern's for those settlers along the creek. They're goin' to be caught, plum centre. When the sheepmen and cattlemen's gunnies get hired, they know what to expect . . . what's comin' to 'em. All the farmers are concerned about's their milk yield an' their potato crop. An' it's *them* that's payin' state taxes.'

'But Winder and Quorrel have planned a way for the law to support 'em, when they move in,' Hark responded quickly.

'You figure on Dow Lineman, or the Boses sellin' their range land? Why, the likes o' them wouldn't even sell their cow farts to sheepmen,' Wonnok countered. 'So how you figure it's goin' to be done lawfully?'

'They'll come through the old Wild Bird range, an' that ain't occupied. There's nothin' an' nobody to stop 'em.'

At the mention of Wild Bird, a nerve twitched in Rube's face. The two law officers exchanged a puzzled frown.

'Do we know who *does* own that Wild Bird ground?' Dub Sewett asked.

Hark shook his head. 'Word has it that someone bought it off a beneficiary o' Malachi Bird. That was a few years back though, an' no one's sure. But if the sheepmen get their woollies onto it, you won't want to be playin' it from the middle. So it'll be the Topeka courts that have to decide what happens. An' that's more'n three hundred miles.'

They continued their gruff discussion, were still at it when, ten minutes later, a group of tough-looking men pushed their way through the batwings. The conversations ceased, the card players held their game and the barman took the whiskey bottle from the counter. Rube wryly congratulated himself on the timing of his arrival, had a long stare into the back bar mirror.

Two of the half-dozen men walked to within six feet of Rube, stood either side of him. From their reflections, Rube recognized them both as having stood watching from the sidewalk on the other side of the street when he'd arrived.

A short, pug-faced character started his broad jaw working. 'Don't I know you?' he growled out. 'We met somewhere?'

Rube studied the last of his salt beans, pushed his empty glass across the mahogany for another refill. It wasn't a move to appease the man.

'Hey, I'm speakin' to you,' the pug man said, more aggressively. 'You got somethin' to do with the cattle-men around here? You in their employ?'

Rube turned to face the man. He shook his head, gave an icy smile.

The other man saw the impending danger for his colleague and butted in. 'My name's Clete Winder,' he said. 'We're runnin' some big flocks into the valley. Rush here's a mite proddy over cowmen's hired guns.'

'Well, I *ain't* one of 'em,' Rube said, short and sharp.

'Just who *are* you, feller?' Marshal Sewett asked, noted Rube's tooled gunbelt. 'Can't be too sure, in these troubled times.'

'I'm someone who's tendin' my own,' Rube answered. 'Name's Cassidy.'

Winder looked hard at Rube. If it turns out you ain't Simon Pure, mister, you can bet we'll meet again. I remember faces.'

'An' where're you from, Cassidy?' Sewett demanded this time.

'North,' Rube answered unhurriedly.

'That narrows it down some,' Wonnok contributed with a sly smile. 'Did you know, you rode smack into the start of a range war?'

'No, I didn't, Sheriff. I thought I mighta been ridin' away from one. I been workin' for Ansel Tribune up around Cedar Springs.'

Winder took a long hard look at Rube, pointed his finger with an implicit threat. Then, with the man called Rush, he walked from the saloon. They were followed closely by their well-armed colleagues into the street.

Dub Sewett grinned at Rube. 'I was wonderin' what they wanted. I'd be *real* careful if I was you, Cassidy,' he advised.

Rube held up a hand in concession to the marshal's well-intended warning. Then he walked over to the batwings, cast a wary eye along the street. 'I'll be wavin' goodnight to the sheepmen,' he said, loud enough for the lawmen to hear.

'Weren't there some trouble up at Cedar Springs?' Sewett asked Wonnok surreptitiously. 'A couple o' years back?'

'Yeah, had 'emselves a sheep problem. An' from what I recall, it was Ansel Tribune who was mixed up in it, too.'

'It's where Orlick must have recognized Cassidy from,' Sewett deduced. 'Winder knew enough not to get involved with him. There was a heap o' bodies left behind, I heard that much.'

Hark turned an interested eye on the two lawmen. 'Easy enough to check it out,' he said. 'It'd be some sort of irony if they'd all been chased out o' border territory by Cassidy, only to run into him again down here. Now, *that's* a squirrelly tale.'

'Don't go settin' it up just yet,' Wonnok advised. 'I'll give he's a man who looks like trouble, but somehow, I don't think he's here to make it.'

Out in the street, the six sheepmen were on their way out of town. Taking point, Clete Winder nodded almost imperceptibly, threw a menacing glance at Rube as he rode past.

From beneath the saloon's porch, Rube watched the riders kicking dust for a moment, before shrugging and turning away.

'Have you seen my pa in there?' a tidily dressed girl asked breathily, as she suddenly appeared on the sidewalk beside him.

Rube raised a finger to the brim of his hat, looked into the girl's dark eyes. 'Er, sorry, miss,' he said, trying to get a general picture. 'The family resemblance ain't strikin' me at the moment. Who exactly is your pa?'

'He went in as Louis Hark, owner of the *Broadcast*. He'll more than likely come out as Big Billy Hell.'

'Oh him, yeah. Now I know who you mean. He's at the bar talkin' some sort o' trespass with the law. You want I should get him for you?'

The girl thought for a moment before shaking her head. 'No. No need,' she said, peering over the batwings. 'I just like to know where he is.'

'Well, if you're sure, ma'am,' Rube said with a smile, tipping his hat once again.

2

SQUARING UP

Peeler and Walt Bose stood side by side under the overhang of the Running Steer Saloon. They were the owners of the Lone Tree ranch. Near them was Dow Lineman, the owner of Red Iron. It was the sheepmen leaving Cuffy Deke's that had caught their attention.

Peeler punched his right hand into the palm of his left. 'There's a missed opportunity,' he said, as they watched the sheepmen ride from town.

'Unless we chase after 'em,' Walt suggested mischievously.

The men stood and speculated on what had happened in the nearby saloon, got more curious as people congregated on the sidewalk outside. Peeler muttered for his brother to look up, as Digby

Wonnok turned and walked towards them.

The brothers glanced at Dow Lineman, waited for the sheriff who was now accompanied by Dub Sewett.

If you boys are goin' back in, we'll join you,' Wonnok said, with an encouraging grin, indicated that the cattlemen re-enter the Running Steer.

Through the throng of carousing cowboys, the group pushed their way to the bar.

'You fellers must be bustin' for a press release,' Wonnok said, and called for a bottle of whiskey.

'Yeah, we did wonder,' Peeler answered. 'Are them mutton punchers your new drinkin' companions?'

Wonnok grinned. 'Did you see that feller who came out behind 'em? He watched 'em leave.'

'I saw him,' Walt said. 'He somebody special?'

The sheriff recalled the sheepmen's accusation that Rube Cassidy was in the pay of the cattlemen. 'It was on *his* account they left, 'an there was six of 'em,' he said. 'That makes him pretty special, I guess. His name's Rube Cassidy. Maybe you heard of 'im?' The Boses and Lineman shook their heads.

'There was a snappy one who accused Cassidy o' throwin' in with you lot. Greasy Quorrel saved him from spendin' the rest of his life as a cripple,' Wonnok informed them.

For the next few minutes, the cattlemen listened to Sewett and Wonnok's account of the goings on in Cuffy Deke's. Not completely trusting, Wonnok angled to connect them with Rube, but there was nothing to confirm the suspicions of the sheep-men.

When they heard of Louis Hark's theory that someone had bought up Wild Bird, Peeler Bose expressed a thought. He turned to Dow Lineman.

'You ain't secretly gone an' taken over that land have you?' he asked him.

Lineman shook his head. 'No. I never figured I'd need more range,' he declared. 'There was a time though, a few years back. I was in Topeka . . . looked into the records. I notioned the land could be picked up for next to nothin' if there was owed taxes. But they'd been paid up.'

Peeler gave Lineman a sharp look. 'How'd you mean? If the taxes have been paid, it means there's a beneficiary . . . someone owns it.'

'I thought there was only three members o' the Bird Family,' Walt put in. 'Them that lived there, anyways.'

'You mean them that died there. There is three graves,' Lineman added.

Wonnok drained his glass. 'We know there's some-thin' here don't square, gentlemen. But I've already said what I think about the chances o' cowmen sellin' land to sheepmen.'

'Where does that leave us then?' Walt asked.

'If anyone does move onto that land before we know for certain, me an' a big bad posse'll scuttle 'em back a lot further than where they came from,' the sheriff threatened.

Peeler took a step away from the bar. 'Thank you for the drink, Sheriff, but me an' Walt got a long ride back.'

'Yeah, guess I'll be moseyin' along too,' Lineman said.

'Be seein' you,' Sewett responded without further ado, as Wonnok refilled their glasses.

Outside of the saloon, Walt Bose followed his brother and Lineman, along to where their horses were hitched.

'What was all that about?' he asked them, looking around, half hoping to spot a loose sheepman.

'I think it was the law wantin' to know where we stood on the employ o' gunfighters,' Peeler said.

'Yeah,' Lineman agreed, 'perhaps we should've. If them sheepguts got some kind o' claim on the old Wild Bird range, how we goin' to keep 'em out? It sounds like they're movin' real fast.'

'They ain't there yet. To stop 'em, me an' Walt'll run our own cattle across the south fork. Just see if we don't,' Peeler warned.

'Who the hell is this Cassidy feller, then?' Walt wondered, as Lineman pondered a moment.

Peeler shrugged as they walked on. 'I don't know. Perhaps he's a dip salesman. You said you hadn't heard o' him, Dow?' Peeler queried.

'That's what I said, yeah. But I think I have. Don't rightly know where or when. I'm wonderin' how Quorrel's man knew him. Perhaps they all been monkeyin' around where they shouldn'ta been.'

'Why don't we find Cassidy an' ask him?' Walt suggested. 'From what Wonnok said happened in Cuffy Deke's a cinch he ain't bedded down with 'em.'

Peeler nodded his approval. 'We'll go an' look for him . . . tell the boys to ride back,' he said.

It didn't take long for the three of them to discover that Rube Cassidy wasn't in town.

'Strikes me, it could be *you* gets hurt first and worst, Dow,' Peeler said, as they sat their horses, having checked at the livery. 'Do you reckon you can run some cattle on to Wild Bird?'

'Ha! Do skunks smell 'orrible? I'll put some grown stuff over as soon as I can. I ain't goin' to be left out o' this.'

'We'll meet you there, Dow,' Peeler promised.

'Good, 'an I just thought o' somethin' else,' Lineman said. 'Them sheep up north o' the ridge? Well it's a ruse. There ain't enough of 'em. The big numbers are closer to Wild Bird. They'll be spread along the foothills, an' they're goin' to have to be stopped.'

'Sounds better than drivin' a herd o' cows. Maybe I'll get me that dustin' after all,' Walt enthused.

'You'll get *that* all right,' Peeler said. 'But we'll stand off and use rifles. If Quorrel an' Winder are surrounded by paid gunnies, we don't want any of

16

our boys hurt 'cause we ain't been circumspect now, do we?'

'No, we certainly don't want that, Brother,' Walt agreed, with a slight, quizzical look.

'I've had another thought,' Lineman said.

'What's it this time, Dow?'

'Maybe this Cassidy feller's been hired by Amis Ralf to look out for Snakehead.'

'No, not likely. Ralf ain't borderin' on trouble right now. An' he wouldn't go it alone without tellin' one of us,' Peeler said. 'But I would like to know what the man's doin' here though,' he added thoughtfully, as he wheeled his horse south for the Lone Tree ranch.

3

WILD BIRD

Ten miles south of Coolidge, Rube rode into the Cimarron Valley. East of the Buzzard Peaks, it was lush Kansas land that hugged the margins of Colorado and Oklahoma. There was a far bigger settlement than he'd expected, but no more than his father had seen coming, many years before.

An hour after sundown, pin pricks of yellow light gave form to the distant homes. The county marshal was right, but Rube was still surprised to see farm buildings flanking the south bank of Ten Mile Creek. Skirting Springfield Ridge, they extended eastward to the twin forks of the creek and the fringes of the Wild Bird ranch, then on to the wooding stations of the Arkansas River.

The stars were bright and the moon was at full wax as Rube crossed the creek onto rangeland that hadn't seen cattle for many a year. The Wild Bird was a big wedge-shaped section of territory that was protected by natural boundaries. But only from men who recognized the rights of others. Greasy Quorrel and Clete Winder weren't the first sheepmen to cast grabby eyes on that range and to try taking it.

Rube rode slowly in at the old ranch. During the past years of neglect, the roads and trails had overgrown with wild plants and grass, until they were totally buried. The run of sheds had fallen apart, and pole corrals had perished, rotted into the ground. The long house facing the creek was built wholly of stone, but its roof had buckled and all windows and doors were gone.

In knee-high weeds in front of the barn, Rube brought his mare to a stop. For a minute or so, he levelled his gaze towards the home side of the creek's north fork. He knew that on rising ground, and beneath a grove of blue beech, there were three headstones. They were the graves of the Bird family, shot dead by the sheepmen.

There was no change in Rube's flinty expression. He'd got work to do, wasn't going to dwell on a cheerless past. He reasoned that as soon as Quorrel and Winder got themselves moved out of Coolidge, they'd be riding on to Wild Bird land. He moved slowly around the old barn, then he turned east, rode to the base of Springfield Ridge.

Rube headed for an old track that began a mile beyond the ranch, though now it was no more than a scar over the high wall up which it led. But, despite the years since he'd last ridden it, he knew the trail well. He eased the roan through the shallow scree, and then for a half-hour more, climbed steadily to the low timber that capped the sharp rising slope. He found the cover he was seeking in a fissure, and drew in to unpack and rest. With his back against a gnarled and stunted pine, he ate a strip of jerk, sweet onions and a corn dodger, washed it down with a mouthful of tepid canteen water.

A short while later, Rube walked to the rim of the ridge, gazed out into the blue-black shadows of the ranch land. The scent of sweet clover drifted up, but nothing pierced the night except the flicker of a dying fire.

As he looked down on what was meant to be a hideaway camp, Rube spat contemptuously. They were sheepmen far below him, and they'd already staked out the western approach to the Wild Bird. Rube's gut tightened as he realized the sheepmen had been ready to move, the day that he'd ridden into Coolidge.

The far north side of the creek fork was choked with virgin timber. Beneath the western escarpment where he now stood, open clearings were dashed with sandy steeps that had collapsed from the wall of the ridge. Around them, concealed by a growth of low thicket were scattered the bleached bones of sheep. Rube couldn't see them, but he knew they were there. The dumb animals had attempted to overrun the Wild Bird. Most of them had been killed with rifle fire, but many of them had formed a terrified gather, and suffocated to death.

Rube backed off from the rim. There was no evidence yet of sheep breaching either the north or south forks of Ten Mile Creek. He thought it might be possible to keep them out single-handed, depending on how near the incoming flocks were, if the men who already occupied the western end of the Wild Bird, got help in time.

Back at the gnarled pine, Rube pulled of his boots and rolled himself first in his blanket, then his slicker on the ground. Such was the ache from his physical and mental tiredness, that he fell almost immediately into sleep. The day had been a long one, but he woke soon after two o'clock. It was near enough to the hour he'd selected as his eyes had closed.

Rising, he ate more jerk and another dodger. For a moment he considered kindling a small fire to make coffee, but decided to do without. He saddled the roan, started the walk back down the ridge.

Rube led his horse around the foot of the ridge. He avoided the shrubs and weeds, until he got closer to where the sheepmen's camp was hidden. There were still no sounds, but although the moon was now down, the stars afforded him some visibility. He slipped the bridle for the horse to graze, lifted the .45 Winchester from its saddle-boot.

Out over the Red Hills, the eastern horizon was just starting to lighten, and Rube advanced warily. Three saddle horses and a pack horse were hobbled in a clearing that was surrounded by dense brush-wood. The animals lifted their heads and smelled him, then returned to their graze. Quietly, Rube went around the clearing, until the gleaming ripples of Ten Mile Creek appeared beyond. The camp was set against the south bank, Wild Bird side. Near to their riding gear, three men were asleep, and snoring noisily.

Rube weighed up the situation, grinned to himself and backtracked to the horses in the clearing. In a few minutes he'd removed the hobbles, tossed them into the darkness and walked the horses towards the foot of the ridge. He knew that if the horses contin-ued north, they'd end up running straight back to their home ground. Rube guessed that wouldn't be too far from Coolidge.

Rube watched the pale-blue light spread slowly across the Kansas sky, as he considered his predica-ment. Having sent the horses packing, he could now do the same to the sheepmen. If he wasn't going to kill them, he'd have to come up with a decent threat, or offer a dark future. He hunkered between two low-spread willows, pulled the brim of his hat down, and decided to wait.

A little over an hour later, Rube's eyes were shaded from the burgeoning sun. He sniffed at the drifting smoke, heard the noises raised by the sheepmen as they busied themselves around their fire. A man carrying feed bags passed close by, and Rube sucked in his breath, waited for him to return.

A moment later, the expected shout came from the clearing. The man came running back, dashed straight to his camp which was ahead and to the right of where Rube was hiding.

'Hey, get up. The damned stock's took off,' he yelled.

Another voice opened with a few curses. 'They're crow-hobbled, Maggs. They ain't goin' far. We'll get 'em back after chow.'

Tin plates were already clattering when Rube thumbed a cartridge into the breech of his Winchester. He walked quietly to within twenty feet of their breakfast fire.

'Those horses are south o' the creek by now, an' you goddamn lamb lickers are in real trouble,' he called out, levered the trigger guard for effect.

The three men rocked forward onto their knees, but didn't turn around.

'You all get yourselves stood up,' Rube went on. 'Drop your gunbelts, an' step away from 'em. Stay lookin' east.'

Wordless, the three followed Rube's orders, moved to one side of the fire. Rube stepped up behind them. He scooped up the holstered Colts and cartridge belts and tossed them over to where he'd been standing.

'Now, let's get ourselves introduced,' Rube said, levelling the rifle as the men turned to face him.

It's the cowpoke from town,' Rush Orlick rasped, after a short moment. 'He's the one I been tellin' you about . . . wears a fancy Mex gunbelt.'

The dirt-scruffed faces of the other two men studied Rube with a mixture of curiosity and concern.

'What game you pullin' down?' one of them asked, uncertain of Rube's back up.

'You're a mile or two off your bedground.' There was clear warning in Rube's response.

'Not us, feller. This here's goin' to be sheep country, which kind o' gives us constitutional rights.'

The nerve in the corner of Rube's left eye twitched again. 'There's a heap o' bones not too far from here that explains "constitutional rights",' he said derisively. 'You men workin' for Wilder or Quorrel?'

'Both. So what?'

'It could be your way of stayin' alive.'

'You goin' to do to us what you did to them boys up near Cedar Springs?' Rush Orlick asked nervously, out of his flat jowly face. 'I've remembered who you are.'

Rube shifted the gun's muzzle a little higher. 'Then you'll remember they had their chances an' preferred to die,' he rasped. 'But you, I'm goin' to move on . . . like goddamn stubble jumpers. Get your boots off, all o' you.'

'We ain't hoofin' it across this country,' Orlick declared.

Rube's finger moved very slightly on the trigger, but the explosion was sudden and violent, made him blink. 'Sorry, I ain't that good with a rifle,' he muttered, grinned malevolently, as the slanting

24

bullet tore up through the brim of one of the other men's hats.

'You might regret not shootin' us, mister,' the man said, grinding his teeth, doing what he was told.

'If you ever make it out o' this place, it'll be *you* regrettin' it, take my word,' Rube countered.

He got them to pile more brush onto their cook fire, waited until the meats were black and charred remains, then, into it went their boots. He made them pare down to their grimy underclothes, and all that followed, until the flames pranced high and colourful. With his rifle in one hand, and his Colt in the other, he walked the wretched, cursing bunch back along the creekside to the foot of Springfield Ridge.

'Go find your stinkin' sheep, an' run south with 'em. If I even get to smellin' you again, I promise you won't get such gentle handlin'.' There was no doubt that Rube's telling was sincere and unconditional.

He watched them go, headed for their punishing walk across the rangeland. The heat would increase during the day, become crippling as the sun climbed. 'Good,' Rube said to himself, and made his way back to their camp.

He retrieved the gunbelts from where he'd thrown them. They were all plain cavalryman, from which he emptied cheaply made .36 Colts. He tossed them into the surging flames, was hurrying to his grazing roan when the cartridges began to explode.

Rube pushed the rifle back into its boot, started

back up the narrow file to his hideout perch, high on the ridge.

An hour later, and returned to his gnarled pine, he stared unhappily at the dried beef. He was safe for a while though, and decided on a fire and hot coffee. He knew that trackers would eventually come, that his threats wouldn't amount to a hill of beans if Rush Orlick and his partners returned with half an army. They'd start looking for him in the upper end of the valley, before realizing he'd taken to higher ground. Eventually, they'd discover his trail from the base of the ridge so, sometime during the day, he'd have to find an alternative vantage point. Meantime, he'd soak until mid-morning, then take a look out from the rim.

4

TAKING THE SHEEPMEN

No one showed until an hour before noon. Rube was expecting some action from beyond the ridge, was surprised by a bunch of riders approaching Wild Bird land from the north. Carried by the breeze, the heard the clink of tack over the soft pounding of hoofs. The men rode tight, and Rube guessed they were from Red Iron, that it would be the rancher, Dow Lineman out front.

They followed the creek, turned east below Rube and made for the camp. There was no smoke now, but the tang of burned boot leather blew low through the brush. The men drew rein and, within fifteen minutes, four of them were following the tracks of the sheepmen's hired guns. They went where they should, where Rube expected them to, south beyond the ridge into the rise of Buzzard Peaks. The others made a resting site beneath a willow brake along the north fork of the creek.

Rube stared out across the scope of Wild Bird's range, remembered the Coolidge newspaperman's words about the dangerous and unstable gather of cattlemen and sheepmen.

The second group of horsemen didn't come out the blue. Rube saw them through the creek timber, and long before he caught their sound. He counted ten, and they were being led by Walt and Peeler Bose. They followed the trail of the Red Iron cowboys until they met at the temporary camp. A thin, disturbing smile cracked Rube's face. Without a doubt, there was more in the offing than a cattlemen's association meeting.

It was late afternoon when the Red Iron riders returned from their trailing of Rush Orlick south from Springfield Ridge. Rube had a few moments of concern, wondered if they'd start over, find his rising track. But, after they'd parleyed, the combined force headed out fast and determined through the south-western end of Wild Bird.

'You found sheepmen,' Rube muttered. He turned from the rim, struck his meagre camp and saddled the roan.

Cautiously, he rode the ridge trail back to the valley floor, hugged the slopes before rising again into the foothills of the Peaks. He spotted no other rider as he continued further south, climbing higher into dense timber. He rode on to a spur of projecting rock, could still see no sign of the cattlemen's force below him.

He moved off again, zigzagging through the aspen and pine. He figured out the riders were close to the edge of the Peaks. But they were still moving south of the valley. He walked the roan, checked frequently for any sign of distant movement.

The sun was falling into the western horizon, nudging the distant Rockies, when the crackle of gunfire split the heavy silence of the range. From the edge of the timberline far below him, disturbed scrub jays took to the air as Rube hauled in the roan.

The opening shots quickly rolled into a crescendo. A relentless pattern of gunfire that crackled for ten minutes before the first let-up. The noise didn't cease completely. It faltered, trailed off further to the south around the curve of the slopes.

'They sure found somethin',' Rube said to his horse, rubbing its forehead. He kicked his heels, moved the roan quicker through the trees. He wanted to get further along the timberline, find a vantage point where he could see what was happening.

It was the sheepmen he saw first. They were holed up, spread along a rocky spine that broke from the Peaks. They were desperately fending off the cowmen, trying to stop them from getting to their stock.

But the attack was now coming two-pronged. One small group of sheepmen had already been hit as they'd held up their panicky animals. Another group was taking cover behind one of their camp wagons, returning fire at the advancing cattlemen. Beyond them, further east into the range, herders were trying to string some sheep up towards the lower creek, its shallow crossing, that would take them onto Wild Bird land. Two sheepmen were making their way back towards the ridge. They had escaped the fire of the cowmen, were on foot, clambering through the tumble of rock and scree.

Rube continued his watch, noticed the sheep kills. They were lying half a mile from the shelter of the rocky spine, piled in small heaps where they'd clumped in their panic. It was where the fighting had started, where Dow Lineman and the Bose brothers had met up with the sheepmen.

Most of the killing had been dealt with at long range, by rifles. But now the attacking force was closing in. The bigger outfit was now using pistols, as they circled the rocky spine, cut it off from the wagons.

Rube could see the sheepmen grabbing their horses, beginning a retreat into the brush between their scant cover and the start of the timberline.

Hidden from all but a high circling vulture, Rube looked down on the rout. 'Bet none o' them fought at Bull Run,' he muttered scornfully.

The sheepmen were fearful and disorganized.

Their flight to the Peaks was devastating as the cattle-men's fire cut them down. A hundred or more sheep got away from a frightening death, but many more were left abandoned.

For a fleeting moment, the gnaw of cordite whispered its way high into the foothills, caused the roan to whicker.

'Easy, girl. Better smoke in this world than in the next,' Rube said, quiet and calmly. The sheepmen were now out to save themselves as first dark arrived. There was no more gunfire, as they scattered. For a half-hour there was hardly any sound, then Rube heard the crackle of burning wood. Two wagons had been set ablaze, with tongues of bright flame rising to the darkening sky. Then he saw the fast-moving, small, shadowy figures, heard the resurgence of rapid gunfire.

The cowmen were killing the sheep. They were shooting them as fast as they could, would continue until they ran out of ammunition. Any remaining animals would hurtle unthinkingly for the strong-hold of the Peaks or the open range beyond the settlements. It would be many days before the herders gathered them in, if ever.

Rube stared into the night sky, then closed his eyes for a moment. He let the memories of Cedar Springs return, his last involvement with sheep-men. Once, he'd done what the cowmen far below him were doing now, had had to. The destruction of any livestock didn't sit well with him, but he

31

knew it was the only way. Quorrel and Winder would use their sheep as an invasion force, an assault weapon to munch its way across the entire Cimarron Valley.

Whatever was happening on the range below him, Rube knew the sheepmen would return more overbearing, more forceful. He felt the icy run of sweat between his shoulder blades and shivered, knew there'd be a lot more death before any sort of peace settled on cattle country.

5

AN UNDERSTANDING

Long after the last gun's echo cracked out, and until the wagons were no more than charred embers, Rube contemplated his prospects. It was well into full dark now, no need for any more hiding. He climbed on to the roan, and for an hour he backtracked north.

Within sight of Springfield Ridge he made himself a camp, enjoyed scalding coffee. In the early hours he fell asleep with a twisted smile of irony on his face. He was head counting the stock that would soon be coming down from Cedar Springs.

At sun up, he cooked a mixed skillet of salt pork, canned tomatoes and crumbled pone. It was the last of his provisions, a relative feast. He packed leisurely, and looked out to where he was headed. It was north to the ridge, then west through the settlements, on to the Red Iron and across the creek to Wild Bird.

Tugging at the horn of his saddle, Rube saw the distant trail line of slow-moving cattle. He held his hat against the rising sun, squinted to make out detail.

This can't be 'em. Not from that direction, he thought. Not from Cedar Springs. Must be a Red-Iron drive, on the way to new grass. He had a last quick glance, then mounted up, took the trail to Wild Bird.

Hours later, the roan trampled the thick corn-cockle outside the ranch's derelict buildings. Rube decided to make provisional use of the largest of the stone-walled sheds. He freed his bedroll and traps, unsaddled and set about moving fallen roof timbers. Later, when supplies could be freighted out from Coolidge, he'd do some work on the house and the barn. At noon, he had more thoughts of the Red Iron – why they should be moving cattle. He specu-lated on the possibility of Dow Lineman fording the creek. The more he thought about it, the more he knew he'd have to ride out and take a look.

Rube resaddled the roan, and set off at a deter-mined canter. He rode the willow brakes for an hour until he found the crossing point he was looking for, then the boulder-rimmed scrape that gave him the cover.

Well hidden, Rube sat his saddle, stared across the bright, shallow water into the range. He saw the big herd when they were less than a mile away. And his thoughts were right. The Red-Iron cattle were heading straight for Wild-Bird range.

Two men were riding point, but loop men showed along the flanks of moving cattle. Rube didn't ride out to meet them, he waited patiently while the herd came towards him. The lead steer was less than a hundred yards off when he quit cover, splashed across the creek.

The two riders drew rein, were taken aback when Rube lifted a warning hand.

'You ain't thinkin' o' makin' it across here, are you, boys?' Rube drawled. 'Them beeves are startin' to give off the whiff o' trespass.'

'Yeah, to who? We ain't seen nothin' or nobody.'

Guardedly, Rube moved a hand to the butt of his Colt. '*I'm* sittin' here tellin' you,' he said.

One of riders was about to respond to Rube's confrontation, when two more riders came galloping up from the herd. One of them was Dow Lineman.

'What's the hold up?' he asked. 'Who the hell are you?' when he realized that Rube wasn't one of his own men. The man's features were haggard, worn tired. He scrutinized Rube, remembered the story of a man who'd run up against sheepmen in Coolidge.

Rube gestured at the cattle. 'Looks like your boys were set to stroll 'em on to my land. I sure wouldn't take too kindly to that.'

'Your land?' Lineman queried, his interest turning suddenly to unease.

35

'Yeah, mine. So *that'll* be the hold up.'

Lineman's face broke in to a weary grin. 'So, you'll be Rube Cassidy, the man who set them fellers afoot half naked, burned down their camp.'

Not a trace of amusement marked Rube's face as he nodded his head. 'Sheepmen got no business in this part o' the valley, or their hired guns. From what I saw last night, I reckon there's others who feel the same.'

Lineman thought for a moment before saying anything. 'I heard you did some ramroddin' up near the border,' he said, slanting the answer.

'I used to work for Ansel Tribune, if that's what you mean, Mr Lineman.'

The Red-Iron boss held back a smile. 'You don't any more?'

'Nope. An' I'm here on my lonesome . . . aim to bring in a herd.'

Lineman stared, let the smile develop. 'Well, kick my ass,' he exclaimed.

'I just might, if I see a single one o' your beeves on my land.'

'Ha. You ain't playin' some goddamn trick, are you? Just holdin' us up so the sheepmen can take over? You already seen what happened to Quorrel an' Winder.'

'You got to be jokin'. As long as I can pull a trigger, woollies are never goin' to run on Wild-Bird land . . . never,' Rube levelled back at Lineman.

Lineman recognized Rube's uncompromising

stance. From what he'd heard, what he could see, it was obvious the man facing him was no shepherd. He turned to his riders.

'Let 'em spread, boys,' he ordered. 'There's enough green on this side o' the creek to hold 'em.'

Lineman's riders had a look behind them, decided to hang around for a minute or two.

'You plannin' on runnin' an outfit up here by yourself, then?' Lineman asked.

Rube nodded. 'Yeah. But then I ain't talkin' your size bunch. One man can handle the numbers I got in mind. Specially with the natural boundaries o' Wild Bird.'

'You better sleep at the full moon, Cassidy. I'm thinkin' that on some dark night, a sheepman'll sneak in an' stick you to your bed.'

'I guess they'll be tryin'. Like you were, up until ten minutes ago.'

'We had good reason,' Lineman said. 'We wanted a land buffer to protect ourselves against the sheep. They don't call 'em maggots for nothin'. An' you said yourself, the creeks out o' Springfield Ridge are good, natural boundaries.'

'Who's *we?*' Rube asked.

'The Bose brothers. Walt an' Peeler. They're trailin' a herd that ought to be out here sometime tomorrow.'

'Hate to see 'em go to all that trouble,' Rube said calmly. 'I'd appreciate you sendin' word for 'em to disperse or turn around. From now on, what goes for sheep, also goes for any other man's beef.'

Lineman nodded his understanding. 'That's plain enough. I just hope you can keep your hair on straight,' he replied. Face-to-face, he was influenced by Rube's sincerity, his obvious intent. Twisting around in the saddle, he spoke to one of his men. 'Mitt, ride back an' tell Walt an' Peeler to hold up. Don't try explainin'. Just tell 'em I said to.'

The cowboy nodded once, turned his horse south and kicked his spurs.

'Much obliged,' Rube said to Lineman. 'Now, I got me some home improvements to make.' He nudged the roan, walked it to the creek crossing, the way back on to his land.

Lineman watched until Rube had made it to the far side of the creek. 'Wonder how long he'll last?' he muttered.

6

TRAILING STOCK

In the days that followed, Coolidge was shaken by stories of the battle between the sheep and cattlemen. Hundreds of sheep had been trapped, run down and shot dead. Many men had been killed and badly wounded during the long, drawn-out fight. That was the gathering news, reports that were added to daily, as cowboys left piecemeal information in the town's bars, beaneries and boarding-houses.

According to the stories, there was little doubt that the cowmen had gone on the offensive in order to protect themselves. No sheepmen had been seen in town, but again, it was rumoured that Quorrel and Winder were seen in Garden City. They'd been busy with lawyers, making demands for a lawful safe-guard.

It was publication day of the *Coolidge Broadcast* when the news first broke in town. For two days, Louis Hark sought to establish facts from the rumours. For a special edition of his newspaper, he tried to further dramatize events by placing the fight on Wild-Bird land. But considering the parties involved, thought better of it. Due to the lack of other articles, he actually had next to nothing for the regular issue, couldn't make up more than a single broadsheet.

Late one morning, frustrated by the situation, he left his copy desk. He called out to his daughter who was sorting advertisements in the print room.

'Hey, Etta. I'm goin' to try an' run down these rumours. There's got to be factual print, somewhere out there.'

Etta's dark eyes sparkled. 'That's what a good newspaper man would do, Pa,' she said affectionately. 'Call in at the marshal's office. That's always a fount of reliability.'

Hark turned and smiled, wagged a finger at Etta's humour. Within ten minutes, he was sipping whiskey at Cuffy Deke's with Dub Sewett. He expressed his concerns about the lack of reliable witnesses.

Sewett listened politely, then shook his head. 'I don't know any more than you,' he said. 'Maybe not as much as that, even. Along this street, there's as many different stories as there are horse apples. I've learned to step round all of 'em.'

'I got eyes an' ears in the Runnin' Steer. There's not a word been blabbed about what really happened. You'd think the pig's piss they serve in there would turn any cowboy slack jawed,' Hark declared.

'Not if they want to get paid at the end of the month,' Sewett ventured. 'You don't think the likes o' Dow Lineman woulda threatened 'em with that . . . even more?'

'I'm sure he has. But my best news usually comes from someone who can't stop talkin'.'

Sewett puffed his dissent. 'Not this time,' he said. 'An' don't forget, they'll be on fightin' wages. Besides, if you print the truth, it'll read like an unprovoked attack. We got laws against that sort o' thing. Even big-time cowmen know that.'

While Hark stared mystified into the back bar, the Bose brothers and Amis Ralf pushed their way through the batwings. It was a twist of fate that Kalfs eyes were brown and watery, bulged big from a tanned face.

The cowmen acknowledged Hark and Sewett, as they made for the bar. A fresh bottle of whiskey was produced, and more drinks were poured all round.

'Anythin' in what we been hearin' about a big gunfight below the Peaks?' Hark pursued his enquiries.

Peeler Bose gave a dry smile. 'I can understand your interest, Lou, what with bein' a newspaper man an' all,' he answered. 'We all been hearin' a lot

41

o' wild yarns, but so far, none of us seen any evidence.'

'An' what sort of evidence would that be?' Hark asked.

'The dead men. The wounded men. The remains o' battle. You think there'd be somethin' to show for *such* a big fight.'

Hark detected a slight, twisted grin on Walt Bose's mouth, and Kalf was holding a snigger. The newsman knew that no wounded had been brought into town. Nor had the doctor made a recent visit to any of the ranches. He'd checked on that, likewise knew the undertaker hadn't turned a spade.

Hark's frustration welled up still more when Rube Cassidy made his way into the saloon. He was suddenly suspicious that the man who'd appeared to be a drifter was somehow involved with the cattle-men. He watched. Using the cowboys' parlance, thought he'd pick up some sign.

But for Hark, it wasn't to be. Rube didn't order a drink. He approached the cowmen and settled his gaze on the owner of Snakehead ranch.

'You're Amis Kalf? he asked, but it sounded like he already knew the answer.

The dogie-featured man looked steadily back at Rube. 'Somethin' I can do for you?'

'Yep. I've got five hundred head o' she-stuff closin' on your western range. If the boys drivin' the herd have made any kind o' time, we're talkin' sundown. So, I'd like your OK to cross the

42

Snakehead, north o' Ten Mile Creek.'

Kalf shrugged. 'There's a mile-wide stock lane that side o' the creek,' he said. 'You can use it like any other stockman. You don't need my permission.'

Rube nodded briefly. 'An' I *don't* have to be *civil*, either,' he retorted.

'So that's right, what we heard, is it?' Peeler Bose enquired. 'You goin' into the cow business?'

'I'm *in* the cow business,' Rube answered.

'Your own cattle?'

'Yeah, they're my own. Carried the Tribune's mark once upon a time.'

'You sure them ranches up around Cedar Springs ain't spreadin' south?'

A thin smile moved fleetingly across Rube's face. 'That sounds like a pretty way o' sayin' somethin' else,' he suggested. 'I got all them cows the hard way ... took most of 'em as wages from Ansel Tribune.'

'That tallies, Peeler,' Walt Bose spoke up. 'There's vented brands, two, three years old. They been slashed, no attempt to cover. Some's recent.'

Peeler grinned warmly at Rube. 'There you go, feller,' he said. 'We all wish you luck. You're goin' to need it.'

Rube nodded, then thoughtfully turned to Peeler's brother. 'How'd you know about the brands on my cattle?' he asked keenly.

'Some trail hands I took on said they saw 'em.

There's three men drivin' upwards o' four hundred head. They're north-west o' town, slantin' towards the creek.'

Rube whistled, then exclaimed, 'Well, I'll be. They've made good time. I'd better go help bring em in.'

7

MOVING IN

'It's a big parcel o' land all right. But there's too few cows, an' too few hands,' was Peeler Bose's opinion. 'We need an outfit in there, three or four times the size that Cassidy's aimin' to run.'

'He won't last long,' Kalf added. 'Only long enough for a grave reckonin'.'

Marshal Sewett eyed the men with some distaste. 'Cassidy weren't part o' that fight. He saw what happened, but he weren't part of it,' he said.

'Those maggot men don't know that,' Kalf scoffed.

'You fellers come in past the mercantile?' Sewett then asked.

'Yeah, we did. Why?' Peeler asked back.

'You musta seen Jammer Miley's bull train. They was loadin' with a mountain o' stuff. Him an' a couple o' packers. There was everythin' from green lumber to furnishin's an' flour.'

'What you sayin', Marshal?' Peeler wanted to know, after short consideration

'I'm sayin' that Rube Cassidy's bought all that stuff. He's hired Jammer to haul it out to Wild Bird, an' he don't aim to move on.'

'You don't figure Cassidy's strong enough to stand up to the sheepmen?' Louis Hark wondered.

The cowmen regarded Hark amusedly for a moment. Amis Kalf coughed up a short laugh.

'Laugh, you may,' Hark said. 'But he's a cowmen like yourselves. If he falls, before long it'll be settlement land. Sheep don't know the difference.'

'Well it ain't happened yet,' Peeler stated forcefully, and called for another bottle.

On the way out of town, Rube passed the mercantile, saw the last of his goods being lifted from the loading platform. There were three ox wagons already full, and canvas covers were being tied in. Rube estimated his cattle would be arriving on Wild Bird, about the same time.

He left Coolidge, rode north along the border road. He stayed on it, until he saw where the herd would swing east to the stock lane and Ten Mile Creek. He lifted the roan to a gallop, before midday found the herd nooning among timber to the east of Buzzard Peaks.

The three drovers had a pack train of eight extra horses that also belonged to Rube. Two of the men were unknown to him, but the third unbent from where he'd been resting, and extended his hand in greeting.

'Hey, Rube,' he hollered. 'We all made it.'

'Yeah, we all made it, Shave, an' you in real good time,' Rube said, shaking hands and smiling broadly.

Shave Renson said the ride had gone well, as he led Rube over to the young cowboys he'd brought with him. Renson made the introductions, told Rube about Ansel Tribune's message.

'Said I was to make sure you knew your job's still open if you want it.'

'I know it is,' Rube told him. 'But this is somethin' I've spent my growin' years on. Somethin' I've got to do.'

'Yeah. Mr Tribune reckoned you'd still be of a mind. If you make out, he's always got cattle you can make a deal on, Rube, an' he's thrown in twenty head o' range bulls, for goodwill.'

Soon afterwards they moved the cattle out, strung them south to the stock lane. Rube rode alongside his old friend Shave, continuously admired the quality of the short horns.

They made one more night camp on the trail, the next afternoon crossed the north fork of Ten Mile Creek onto Wild-Bird land. Rube pushed them all on to where the north and south forks met, turned them loose within sight of the ranch house.

'So's they'll know where they belong,' he told the Tribune cowboys. After they find that out, they can drift wherever they please.'

The Tribune men were surprised that Wild Bird ranch had been so abandoned. Renson had a good look over the place, recognized its value. He recalled Tribune saying that when Rube had taken off south, he was probably heading for a small outfit, maybe taking up an open-range claim. But Renson could see that that wasn't the case. He knew that Rube had put all his earned dollars into the small, but quality herd. There was some big work ahead, but he knew it would be worthwhile.

Jammer Miley's bull train pulled in at sundown that night. For a safer crossing, the tough oldster had taken the train further down the creek to where it shallowed, crossed within a mile of the home pasture.

At sun-up the following morning, the cowboys helped the packers start to unload the four big wagons. Building materials were stacked between the barn and the dilapidated sheds, the furniture and cooking stove were carried straight into the house.

Late in the afternoon, when the Jammer Miley outfit had gone, Renson decided they'd stay over, rest up awhile before returning to Cedar Springs. Ansel Tribune hadn't set them a particular time for getting back.

'We can help out here, Rube,' Shave offered. 'Fix the roof up, make it watertight at least.'

The men did more than that. First, they set up the stove, enabling them to cook food and stay on a while longer. They cleared the sheds and patched the barn, burned off the rotted corral posts and set new ones. The cattle moved slowly to the east, spread themselves between the natural containment of the creeks.

Of the five rooms in the house, Rube managed to fix up three of them. The immediate ground, in and around the buildings, was also cleared and turned. Rube told the cowboys he'd think of getting himself a couple of sheep to keep the weeds down. Quickly, the ranch began to take on the appearance of a proper outfit, of someone living and working there.

The night before the Tribune cowboys were to leave, Renson glanced thoughtfully at Rube.

'I rode up to them willows at the creek today,' he said. 'Looks like a whole family buried there. Name o' Bird. I guess it was them that built this place.'

Rube nodded his head. 'Yeah, I guess. Now, *I'm* here,' he said, quiet and unrevealing.

'Well it's a mighty fine spread,' Renson adjudged. 'There's good water, timber along the north fork an' plenty o' lush range grass. Long way from trouble too, eh Rube? Looks like the successful trappin's.'

Stay around a while longer and you might not be thinking that, Rube thought. He thanked the men for staying on, for their work. He didn't mention the battle that had already taken place in the sheep and cattle war. Nor did he ask if they were passing through Coolidge on the way home.

*

49

That was what Shave Renson and his two young companions did though. It was at the noisy, crowded bar of the Running Steer, that they heard the unmistakeable murmurings of the range war. They decided to split up and learn more, meet in Cuffy Deke's to consider their findings.

The three men from Cedar Springs were surprised at what was happening in the valley, what had already happened out below Buzzard Peaks. For Rube Cassidy, Renson worried that Wild Bird lay wide open to sudden onslaught. He knew the likely outcome. Something like it had happened once before.

'I'm sorry boys, but there's no time for cuttin' the wolf loose. My old partner Rube's at the heart o' real trouble,' he told his men. 'We're gettin' on home. If Mr Tribune still wants to be of any help, I'm thinkin' there's a way.'

8

GUARD DOGS

Rube knew full well he wasn't a long way from trouble, knew he'd have to give serious thought to the dangers of Wild Bird. He wouldn't leave though, not now he'd got the ranch house patched and some comforts within. He'd remain on his land for as long as possible in its defence against sheepmen. He'd get some geese. They were excellent sentinels, gave harsh alarm of any approach.

He needed to buy stock feed, thought he'd try one of the settlement farms. Maybe they could supply him with some feathery guards as well as mixed grain.

One early morning, not long after the Ansel Tribune men had departed, he walked the roan through the willow brakes, across the south fork of

Ten Mile Creek. The farms were spread east as far as he could see. Squared off plots of corn, beet, potatoes and fruit trees. More distant fields were full of seed-raiding crows.

Most of the homes were neatly painted. Work buildings were in good order, picket fencing neat and tight. At the first farm, he enquired of a man who was tending squash in a garden plot.

'Try the Perrys, why don't you,' the man said tiredly. 'Next along, when you keep to the creek. You can get grain from 'em, they sure got enough.'

The Ase Perry people were the first to journey west of the Red Hills, far into the valley. The entire family worked in the fields, took their share of the ploughing and planting. Perry was a good-natured, chubby man who left his ripper mare, when he saw Rube approaching. He wore hickory shirt and pants and a slouch hat, dabbed some dirt around his meaty face.

Rube introduced himself, said he was in the market for cereal to feed his saddle brokes.

The man took off his hat and replaced it, thought a further moment before responding. 'You live up there?' he asked, inclined his head in the direction of Wild Bird.

'I do. A spread nearly as big as yours,' Rube said, and smiled.

Perry's shrewd eyes didn't move much, but Rube knew they'd done a fair estimation of him. He quickly wondered if the man proposed to stick him a heavy price for the grain.

Finally, Perry smiled back. 'Well, we got plenty o' what you need,' he observed. 'I'm just tryin' to get it through my bone head, that what us poor farmers breakfast on, you big sugars feed to your animals.'

Rube grimaced at the soft mocking. 'The other ranchers are buyin' from you then, are they?' he deduced smartly.

'No, they won't buy from us. They reckon on even more settlers, if there's a market standing by,' the man said regretfully. 'They're content to buy from Coolidge or Garden City at twice the price they'd be payin' us. So, me an' my boys'll haul your feed grain, if you want. What do you say to ten dollars a load? That's about fifty sacks.'

'That sounds like a good deal.' Rube said, considering the remains of his stake. Perry told him to ride around to the barn, where he'd meet him.

Perry's wife and two grown daughters were scything hog-weed close to the barn, smiled shyly when Rube rode up. There were some pointy-eared dogs running around and Rube watched them, interested in their belligerent play.

A minute or two later Perry appeared. He shouted a terse command at the dogs, indicated for Rube to dismount. He showed Rube the granary, the quality of what he was growing. Rube was more than satisfied and mentioned the dogs. But Perry was more interested in clinching the feed deal.

'I'll take a hundred sacks. Fifty each of oats an'

barley,' Rube decided, and was already counting out the bills.

The two men shook hands, and Perry pointed to a smokehouse, midway between the barn and the creek. Rube followed on, heard snuffles and yips, a low defensive snarl when Perry drew the door bolt.

A bare-fanged dog braced itself a few feet away from the inside of the door. Over Perry's shoulder, Rube peered in and discovered why. Beyond the dog was a bitch, with identical dark markings. In the far corner was a pair of plump, heaving pups.

'Jeez, who the hell are those fellers?' Rube asked, backing off a step.

Perry spoke a soothing word and closed the door very gently. 'Pinschers. I got to keep 'em in there a spell,' he said. 'Whelpin' gets the devil into 'em. At these times you don't want 'em near anythin' smaller'n a mountain goat.'

Rube looked suitably impressed. 'Make good guard dogs then?' he enquired.

'Watch dog, herd guard. Don't ever back away from nothin'. You can school 'em too,' Perry said proudly.

'String beans need that sort o' protectin', do they?' Rube said with a dry smile.

Perry returned the smile. 'Wife's from Germany. Her family always had pinschers apparently. Over the years, they've sort o' grown on me. An' they're always faithful, what's more'n some folk.'

'You want to sell 'em?' Rube asked.

'I never want to sell my dogs. But business is business. Find another twenty, an' they'll be on the load tomorrow. In a few months' time, there'll be nobody crossin' them creeks, 'cept you.'

While they discussed the dogs and their feeding routine, Rube wondered if the sheepmen would be prepared to wait those 'few months'. He was thinking that two fully grown pinschers had the beating of geese, when he realized that Ase Perry had something different on his mind.

There was a moment of silence before the farmer spoke. 'Outside o' the mercantile, we heard about fightin' between the sheep and cattle outfits,' he said.

'Did you now?' Rube came back with.

'Yeah, we did. We also heard there was a few sheepmen left bitin' the ground,' Perry continued. 'We got to wonderin' if that was the truth of it. Maybe you heard the same thing, eh Mr Cassidy?'

'Ha. There's folk in Coolidge don't even tell the truth to each *other*,' Rube laughed. 'Anyways, I haven't been to town lately,' he said, as a concession to candour.

Perry knew that was as much as he'd learn from Rube. He remarked that it wasn't long until noon, and invited Rube to stay and eat.

'Thanks. It's right neighbourly, but I got a heap o' chores. Got to build me a kennel, first off,' he said with a smile. He walked back to the barn with Perry, mounted the roan and tipped his hat in farewell.

'Remember, they won't all be thieves that your dogs bark at. Just most of 'em,' Perry advised. 'You'll have the grain by midday tomorrow.'

9

THE GETTING AWAY

Rube rode away from the Perry farm, turned north, back through the creek and into the willow brakes. He was heedless of any immediate trouble when the roan threw its head and ears back, was already going to the side and down when the bullet struck. It caught him high across his front, felt like a pick stoving in his chest as he crashed heavily to the ground.

The roan spooked away from their heading, snorted through the willow, out into the range below Wild Bird's home pasture.

Rube lay on his back. He was hurt and heavily winded, but he pulled his Colt, listened to the grate of his breath in the close silence. The bushwhacker was two or three hundred yards off, somewhere between where Rube lay and the house. It would be a few minutes yet, before he'd get to assess his work. Rube looked down at his chest. 'That was a new shirt. For that, you'll pay, feller,' he cursed.

In the following stillness, a shrike picked up its raucous cry in the branches of the willow. But Rube had already heard the sound of hoofs. It was two horses walking, two killers who were coming towards him.

He gauged their direction, followed the movement as he brought himself to his knees. They weren't visible through the trees, didn't seem to have a precise bearing, but Rube knew the roan's tracks were deep in the soft ground, would be spotted any moment. When the riders did cross the imprints, Rube heard them draw rein. He scuffled sideways, made his way to the water's edge and the root bole of a crumpled willow. Although blood oozed, and he felt the wetness around his middle, he wasn't feeling much pain. That wouldn't be the wound that killed him, he thought.

Rube heard the riders again when they started talking.

'I'm tellin' you, Tek, he's got to be lyin' here somewhere,' a voice faltered. 'The goddamn horse couldn'ta run that far.'

Rube recognized the voice of Rush Orlick, remembered the threat he'd made, the last time he'd seen him.

'How the hell d'you know?' the man called Tek, answered back. 'All this green stuff looks the same up close. An' how'd you know you hit him, even?'

'I hit him all right. He went down like a buffler.'

'He sure did,' Rube mouthed silently and took a deep breath.

The two men shifted their horses cautiously through the timber, kept their distance from the creek. Rube eased himself up from behind the knot of tangled roots to have a look. Now he could see that the man with Orlick was another one of Quorrel and Winder's crew. His name was Tekker Poole, and Rube recognized him from Cuffy Deke's.

Rube let out his breath, hoped they'd come near enough for him to take them both down. That's what he wanted to do, what he'd threatened Orlick with. But they didn't get any closer. They were so sure about where Rube had fallen, they drew their horses round in tight circles.

'I ain't gettin' down,' he heard Orlick say. 'There's snappers in this stuff, probably rattlers too. If Cassidy *ain't* dead, he will be when *they* find him.'

'Yeah. He'd be throwin' lead at us, if he were still kickin'.'

'Let's go,' Orlick decided. 'We'll tell Greasy and Clete it's safe to mosey on in. If we leave 'em long enough, them beeves'll get 'emselves larded to bust.'

Rube gritted his teeth till his jaw hurt. The only reason he had for letting his would-be killers go, was to stay alive. He wondered if it was good enough. The men had obviously been to his house, spotted him coming up from the south, through the creek. That left bushwhack, just about their only safe option. But they didn't know they'd blown it, and it was going to cost them dear in the long run.

Rube made his way to where the willow broke onto the open range land. Ahead of him was his house, and he hunkered down for a moment, held his arms around his middle. There was no sign of Orlick and Poole, and he guessed they were probably riding to the stock lane, before going on up to Coolidge. He wondered whether there were any more sheepmen or their gunnies around, if there'd be a lookout, in case he survived.

Rube reached out and stripped some thin shreds of bark from the tree beside him. He spat and scrunched it all up, gingerly pushed them through the tear in his shirt. 'Goddamn witch-doctor stuff,' he muttered, knowing full well the willow's medicinal properties.

The wound was still aching dully, but after a painful half-hour's walk, Rube saw his ranch house shimmering in the afternoon's heat. He heard a soft snort on the breeze, turned back to see his roan. The mare was making ground on him, was still nervy though, and walked in its own good time.

There didn't appear to be anyone around the ranch or its outbuildings, but Rube waited another fifteen minutes. Then he felt shaky, and he held on to the horn of his saddle, circled wide to the sheds at the rear of the house. It was now late in the afternoon, and other than the shuffling of his corralled riding stock, there was still no other movement.

As he dragged the saddle off the roan, he saw the sign behind the barn. It looked like two riders had paid a visit, the boot marks showing that Orlick and Poole had had a good look around.

Rube made a fire in the scullery, heated up a kettle of water. He cleaned his wound, was satisfied that it was nothing more than a flesh wound, more gore than grief. Struggling into his other shirt, he went to get his rifle from the barn. He noticed the animal ointments and disinfectants he'd purchased at the mercantile, thought a moderate dash of carbolic wouldn't do him any harm.

Back in the house, he was going to cook a meal, but he suddenly felt sick, and the tiredness had him captured. Cradling the rifle, he lay down on a cot outside of the scullery, and closed his eyes.

It was close to midnight when Rube woke. He lurched to the front door and threw the bolts, saw the mighty canopy of stars in the darkness of the valley.

His chest was tight, and he was sore, but the bad pain had subsided. Not feeling particularly hungry, he went back and made coffee, opened a small can of sweet condensed milk.

Reflecting on what he'd heard earlier, Rube decided that Orlick had meant the sheepmen could occupy Wild Bird at their leisure. It wasn't going to be that night, or even the next day. With Rube lying dead out by the creek, Quorrel and Winder could stroll in. And, free from the fear of attack, they'd fetch the sheep. But that could be another mistake, give Rube time to consider a plan for his ranch's defence.

He went to his bedroom and heeled off his boots, spooned the last of the milk, before succumbing to another sleep.

The rising sun slanted through the easterly windows. It was near eight o'clock when Rube climbed achily from his bed. He cursed at the stiffness, flexed his neck and arms.

He rekindled the fire and gave his wound some more attention. To his relief, there was no fresh bleeding, and he carefully fashioned a clean dressing. Then, he munched on a carrot while considering the stuff of a working breakfast.

An hour later, he sorted himself a sure-foot mare, rode out to where the Bird family graves were sited. The rising ground afforded him a watchful sweep from Springfield Ridge in the west, to near the Arkansas River in the east.

Nothing except his small herd of grazing cattle moved across the land. Then, just before noon, two wagons emerged from the timber on the near side of Ten Mile Creek. True to his word, Ase Perry was bringing his grain in.

Rube went to meet his visitors, gently heeled the mare from the shady grove of beech trees.

10

RUNNING CLOSER

The two dogs and their pups were on the first wagon which was driven by Ase Perry. His two sons were driving the second. Rube bade them good day, rode alongside as they crossed his home pasture.

'Someone followin'?' the farmer asked, noticing that every now and again Rube looked back at the creek.

'No, not followin'. They've been an' gone,' Rube answered enigmatically, the pain still tight across his ribs.

Out front of the barn, Perry braked up, nodded back towards the dogs. 'You watch 'em now, don't get bit. Don't look 'em in the eye just yet, an' don't show 'em your teeth. The bitch we call Frau, and the dog's Hans.'

For a moment Rube didn't understand. Then, as

he dismounted, he smiled stiffly when he realized what was happening. Unless Perry was bringing the parents for a ride, it looked like he was about to take on the whole pinscher family. He wondered again if Perry was a shade wilier than he looked, if so, he'd want more than the twenty dollars Rube had paid supposedly for the pups.

The dogs were leashed securely on top of the sacked grain. They both gave throaty growls, laid back their ears when Rube approached. He stood off a few feet, let them get used to him being there and the smell of him.

He moved around to the back of the wagon and reached tentatively for the pups, shuddered at the mother's warning snarl. He took a deep breath when he saw the stretch of the rawhide leashes, but he scooped up the pups and, with one in each arm, carried them to the house.

Outside of the scullery, Rube stared at the cot he'd used for a few hours the previous evening. Bit by bit, he kicked it to near the door of his bedroom, gently lay down the drowsy pups. Then he pared some beef shin, looked around for suitable dishes.

When he went back to the wagons, the Perrys were already unloading, packing the sacks into the barn.

'You got to handle the mister an' missus now,' one of the boys said.

Rube thought he detected mischief, and he threw Ase Perry a fitting glance. But he'd already decided that he wasn't going to split up the pinscher family.

After a long, intimidating minute, he carefully unfastened the rope from around Frau's neck.

'I've given 'em their own cot,' he shouted, as the mother bounded straight from the wagon to the house.

Hans's body muscle rippled, and an upper lip curled around a spiky canine.

'Good, he's smilin',' Rube said, and untied the leash from the running rail of the wagon. Hans jumped to the ground at his feet, and Rube quickly grabbed the leash, held the dog tight, until he got inside the house.

Frau was sniffing around her pups, nudging them aside for her own cot space. Rube let Hans go, stood watching the proceedings, as it quartered the small room, became familiar with a new home.

Rube laid two plates of meat on the floor, and took his leave. He closed the door, returned to help the Perrys finish the unloading of his grain. A half-hour later, they were all sitting around the kitchen table, dunking hard biscuits in strong coffee.

'Looks like them sheepmen are headin' this way,' Ase Perry remarked, the meaning implicit in his voice.

'You could be in Nebraska, an' headed this way. It's *how far* they get, that interests me. So, tell me what you know.'

'They've pushed at least another two big flocks

an' a covered wagon around the Peaks. Right now, they're movin' through the west end o' Red Iron.'

Rube looked part interested. 'That's Dow Lineman's problem. Why should it interest me?' he asked.

'Pretty soon, there's only goin' to be the south creek between you. Also, they've got a couple o' bells with 'em. 'Cept these are wearin' long coats an' silver badges.'

Rube then more fully understood. One of Perry's boys who'd seen the move, reckoned the sheep could reach the crossing along Ten Mile Creek before nightfall. It was obvious the sheep were being safe-guarded by law officers. If not, Rube suggested, Red Iron or Lone Tree would have hit them the minute they'd reached cattle range.

'Hit 'em *again*, you mean,' Perry said.

Rube half smiled, almost agreed. Quorrel and Winder would be marching on his land in the belief that he wasn't there to defend it. No doubt, they'd been told, by Orlick and Poole, that he was turtle feed.

'How do them dogs feel about sheep?' he asked. 'Cause right now that's all the help I got, if they decide to make a move on Wild Bird.'

In shifting a heavy sack around, Rube's wound had partly opened. He cursed when he looked down, saw a thin line of fresh blood had squeezed across his chest. He shivered, muttered something

66

about the evening chill, before donning a bleached duster.

It was late afternoon when the Perrys went to rehitch their teams, and Rube went with them. He rode most way to the creek, before bidding them farewell.

'Got to get me a good look at them sheep,' he said matter-of-factly. 'You brought good grain an' I thank you for it. By the way, them pups are goin' to be called Fiero an' Paj. Come an' see 'em some time.'

Perry waved. 'You goin' to burn mutton?' he called out.

'That's up to them,' Rube shouted back. He was still wondering what sort of deal he'd got with the pinschers.

Rube waited for the Perrys' wagons to ford the creek, then he followed on. He waited by the fallen willow until almost first dark. It was only then that he saw the roil of dust from the approaching sheep. They were in two main flocks, the furthest still a ways off. The leaders were headed his way, hugging the broken timber along the south fork. There was a sheeted wagon, with four saddled horses, tied alongside. The riders were resting with their backs to the wheels, apparently talking.

Rube knew that to get sheep that far, it would have taken good reason and high-ranking law officers. The two that Ase Perry had seen, would be deputy US marshals at the least. Rube quit the timber, heeled the roan into a canter for the wagon.

He'd covered half the distance when, from his right, a line of riders stepped their horses from the creekside willows. Rube knew immediately it was Dow Lineman and his crew. They'd probably have dogged the sheep near all the way from the Cimarron, then across the western sector of Red Iron land. They'd remained well hidden in the foothills of the Peaks, else the Perrys would have seen them.

Although Rube had been marked since he'd emerged from the timber, not a man moved from alongside the sheep wagon. He rode closer, nudged his roan alongside the tethered horses.

He nodded at the four men, estimated that two of them were sheepmen's hired guns. The other two, wore wide-brimmed hats, had deputy US marshal's badges pinned to their coats. One of them looked inscrutably at Rube, the other seemed slightly irritated. He got to his feet slowly, wanted to intimidate by his bigness.

'You lookin' for somethin'?' he wanted to know. 'We told you cowboys to stay away from these parts.'

'No one's told *me* nothin',' Rube stated. 'An' I'm gettin' real interested in where them sheep are headed.'

'Land 'twixt the creeks. They already tried it once, but got 'emselves shot up. But now, they got us to look out for 'em. You look kind o' confused, feller,' the marshal added, his eyes narrowing as he started to wonder about Rube.

'I ain't confused. I'm concerned . . . riled as to why the law's lookin' out for a bunch o' goddamn landrazin' maggots. They're about to overrun my land, an' from what I've seen, you're abettin' the trespass.'

11

THE OWNERSHIP

The other marshal raised himself from the ground, stood shoulder to shoulder with his partner.

'I'm Jake Fortine, an' that's Parlem Wist,' he said, attempting to read Rube's intent. 'An' *that land's* owned by Greasy Quorrel. Him an' Clete Winder came to Garden City for enforcement. That's what we're doin' here. Now, who the hell are you?'

'Ruben Cassidy. Supposin' there's a difference, Marshal, are you workin' for Quorrel personal, or for the owner o' Wild Bird?' Rube asked.

'Nothin's personal with us,' Wist scowled. 'We come to protect the owner o' the land. See to it they get their rights.'

'Well, your seein's fair, but your hearin's way off. I just told you, Wild Bird belongs to *me*. You got them shiny badges pointed the wrong way,' Rube dug back.

Momentarily troubled, the marshals were looking to each other for a standpoint, when the two gunmen scrambled to their feet and shouted a warning.

From the creekside timber, the Red-Iron crew were approaching at the gallop. The marshals saw them, turned quickly to see that Greasy Quorrel was already leading a large band of men from the opposite direction. Riding with them was Tekker Poole and Rush Orlick. Both men were glaring with shock as they approached, but it was Quorrel who held the crushing displeasure when he saw Rube.

Calmly, Fortine and Wist drew carbines from their saddle boots, walked forward to meet the Red-Iron men.

'You got word, Lineman,' Wist called out. 'Stay away from the sheep, or we'll bring you down. We're empowered to do it.'

'We're here to give Rube Cassidy our support,' Lineman answered. 'He's a cow man, if you didn't know.'

His face set hard with anger, Quorrel kicked his horse forward. 'We need to run sheep, Marshal,' he shouted. 'I seen this drifter in Coolidge,' he added, indicating Rube with his thumb. 'What's he doin' out here?'

'That was somethin' we was just about to get clear, when all you hell-raisers piled in,' Fortine replied. Then he faced Rube. 'You know this man?' he asked.

'I know *about* him,' Rube said. 'Not much more'n a day ago, he thought he'd floated me down to the

Arkansas. That's why he wants to know what I'm doin' out here. I must be a real surprise to him. *Him* an' his hirelings.'

'What's that flapdoodle he's spoutin'?' Quorrel blustered. 'Are you officers gettin' my sheep movin' or not?'

Not one to be harried, Fortine looked to Rube. 'You sayin' they tried to kill you?' he asked, longsufferingly. 'With what you just been tellin' us, mister, you're certainly pilin' on the big windy. Why'd he need to get you wasted?'

'To make his move onto Wild Bird a lot easier. That's why, goddammit. Why don't you turn your attention to them two sittin' quietly behind him? Ask 'em why the hell I'm carryin' a raw gunshot wound under this duster,' Rube answered snappily.

'You'll be wantin' to make a charge against 'em, then,' Wist butted in. 'O'course, you'll have to prove it, an' back in Garden City.'

'There's an alternative. I just ain't thought of it yet.'

'You best make sure I ain't around when you do,' Fortine advised drily. 'Now, what was it you were tellin' us about this land between the creeks?' he asked.

'I own it, an' I got my own cattle in there,' Rube explained, pithily.

Quorrel was infuriated. 'I've had enough o' this,' he raged. 'Let's move.'

Fortine shook his head, and glared. 'That's two

72

people questioned your right to that land, Mr Quorrel. Only this mornin' someone was sayin' they doubted you owned nary a sod. So, to avoid any more confusion, I'm thinkin' we should see some proof o' your title,' he suggested helpfully.

'My deed papers were good enough for the judge in Garden City, an' good enough to get you out here. You don't think I got 'em on me, do you? They're back in my lawyer's office, in Coolidge. Now, Marshal Fortine, I ain't for askin' you again to get my sheep movin'.'

Fortine took a deep breath, turned his attention back to Rube. 'What he says, makes sense,' he suggested as calmly as he could.

'Not to me,' Rube disputed. 'Him, takin' over my land and my house. I've already got a heap of invest-ment up there . . . dependants even. What he's doin', Marshal, is pullin' a big hank o' that sheep wool over your eyes.'

Fortine gave a cruel smile. 'Well, the way I see it, he's got the advantage o' the moment.'

'No, marshal, *I've* got that,' Rube said. 'An' if you're still interested in enforcin' the rights o' the land owner, then I suggest you take a look at this.'

Fortine handed his carbine to Wist when he saw Rube reach beneath his duster. The marshal then moved alongside the roan, took the fold of papers that Rube handed him. In the failing light, he leafed them apart, ran a thumb over the dark smudge of blood. One was a receipt for goods purchased at the

73

mercantile store in Coolidge, the other had two small red seals in a bottom corner. It was a US government land title. Appended was a personal letter written and signed by Ansel Tribune. It read:

This letter testifies that Rube Cassidy has been known to me for many years. For the last five of them, he has been foreman of the Ansel Tribune. During this time, he has taken A.T heifers – including four Poll Durhams – in lieu of a seventy cent on the dollar wage. He is leaving my employ to take his herd of cattle south to the property known as Wild Bird. I attest to all who may come in contact with him, that Rube Cassidy is an honest and law-abiding citizen. Any help afforded him will be well met by me.

Finally, and to whom it may concern:

It will be necessary, and on occasion imperative, that Rube Cassidy implements his real and proper birth name, of Ruben C. Bird.

12

HEADED BACK

Jake Fortine took back his carbine, took a long, hard look at Rube, while Parlem Wist cast an eye over the letter and deed.

'Can't say I know that signature, but no one's goin' to exploit Ansel Tribune's name, I do know that. Not if they value havin' a long an' prosperous life. So, you're actually Ruben C. Bird?' the marshal drawled.

'Yeah, that's me,' Rube said. 'Ain't been called it for nigh on ten years though. As for Wild Bird, I've always owned it.'

Greasy Quorrel spurred his horse closer, his jaw working angrily. 'What the hell you jawin' about?' he demanded. 'You got orders, Fortine. Get on with carryin' 'em out.' Then he reached for the papers. 'Let me see what you got there,' but Wist was handing them back to Rube.

'You really ought to stop tellin' us what to do,' Fortin advised icily. 'I got somethin' else to consider now. Like false swearin' to federal officers.'

'My attorneys have all the proof necessary to establish my rights. You're sellin' out to the goddamn cowmen,' Quorrel railed.

Fortine levered a shell into the chamber of his carbine. 'That's it, Quorrel,' he barked. 'Turn your sheep back. An' for good measure, stay off Red-Iron range.'

Quorrel kicked his horse, angrily wheeled it full circle. 'I ain't got this close just to turn back,' he yelled. 'We're movin' to the creek water, an' I say we'll settle in court.'

'If any one o' you so much as gets a foot wet, I'll deputize every goddamn cowboy here an' run you all the goddamn way to Oklahoma. You goddamn hear me?'

'An' I got pups that'll bite your goddamn ass,' Rube contributed vitally.

The muscles in Quorrel's face and neck trembled with suppressed fury. He saw his time in the valley was up, and he cursed, raked his horse's flanks with his spurs. The Red-Iron crew grinned their scorn as he rode with his men back towards the sheep.

The deputy marshals untied and mounted their horses, rode between Rube and Lineman. Fortine studied the owner of Wild Bird.

'It's all a question o' timin' with you,' he said drily. 'Quorrel an' Winder musta been intendin' to claim

76

occupier's rights. You turnin' up when you did, cut real deep. Musta been an' overridin' temptation to kill.'

'I told you this mornin' Quorrel and Winder didn't own no range,' Lineman said eagerly.

'Yeah, but the Garden City judge was given *some sort* o' evidence by Quorrel's lawyers. An' I hadn't seen that bona-fide deed. If Quorrel and his sheep had got on to Wild Bird, it woulda dragged through the Topeka courts . . . taken years to sort out, an' Quorrel knew it.'

'Probably ended up ownin' it too,' Rube furthered. 'But I'm in now, as long as I can stay alive.'

Lineman was curious. 'You're one o' the Bird family?' he asked. 'A cousin or somethin'?'

Rube shook his head, gave a delayed smile. 'Malachi Bird was my father. I was the one who survived the sheep war o' ten years ago . . . the only one. They rustled an' killed all our cattle. I got away . . . hid up on the Springfield Ridge. I thought they'd come after me, but they never did. They got scared at what they'd done an' scuttled for the border. I didn't know it . . . rode north after payin' a settler to do the buryin'.'

Fortine, Wist and Lineman walked their horses steadily forward as they listened, and Rube continued, 'From that day to this, all I've ever really planned . . . waited for, was to come back to Wild Bird,' he told them. 'Never thought I'd run up against another sheepman. What sort o' broken fortune's that, eh?' Rube rattled through the story as though he was shaking off some of the bitterness he'd harboured.

It was Dow Lineman who voiced an opinion. 'Well, you came back. I reckon we could afford you some help after ten years. Quorrel an' Winder ain't goin' south to graze, or to the Topeka courts, that's for sure. They'll be back.'

'You could do worse than givin' me them papers,' Fortine said supportively. 'I can turn them over to the US marshal. Do that, an' you got surety as far as anyone movin' on to your range is concerned. No judge or marshal's goin' to act for anyone except you, when the proofs locked safely away in a Garden City bank. An' you can keep a copy in Coolidge.'

Rube made a decision that although hard-boiled, both marshals were fundamentally honest. It was a helpful offer from Fortine, and Rube thanked him. There was an original deed issue recorded in some Kansas land registry office, had been ever since his father acquired the land, twenty years ago. But now, it was of little consequence, and Rube didn't know where.

He pulled off the mercantile goods receipt, handed the deed back to the deputy marshal. 'I'm obliged,' he said. 'Now it's a Bird asset, whether I'm alive or dead.'

Fortine smiled. 'I'll mention it to Digby Wonnok. He can inform the town marshal. Now, we got to escort them sheep while we can still see 'em.

Wouldn't do for 'em to get into the foothills. Too many places to hide.'

The men shook hands. Without another word, Fortine and Wist flicked their mounts into a canter, headed south-west to the slopes of Buzzard Peaks.

'Bein' shyster'd by Winder an' Quorrel ain't goin' to sit too well with either o' them marshals,' Lineman remarked.

'They got to offer protection for many a mile yet. They don't want anyone to be at the mercy of Red Iron, do they, Mr Lineman,' Rube suggested, with a glint in his eye.

Lineman accepted the comment with a dry smile. 'For a while there, I figured we were belly down in somethin' nasty,' he said. 'Maybe I shoulda knowed better. You ain't got the stamp or stink o' sheep on you. What were you sayin' about Quorrel's men tryin' to kill you?'

Rube told Lineman about how Orlick and Tekker Poole had attempted to remove him from Quorrel's plan for Wild Bird.

'That's a curious kind o' retribution . . . lettin' 'em ride away,' Lineman suggested.

'You said yourself, they'll be back.' Rube answered with assurance.

Most of the Red-Iron crew had fanned out to keep a watchful eye on the sheep flocks. Lineman yelled for two of the back riders. 'Mitt, you an' Payze are lodgin' at Wild Bird for a few days. Take a string, an' ride 'em hard if you even get a whiff o' mutton.'

Lineman's cowboys waved their acknowledgement, rode fast to select the cavvy mounts. It was timely support and Rube wasn't against their company. In the grip of darkness, the three men then rode for the creek timber and the crossing to Wild Bird. Not for the first time since midday, Rube considered the well-being of his dogs, called on the roan for speed.

13

SHORT STORY

The dogs were quick learners. On returning to the house, Rube was allowed to tousle the pups. Then Hans and Frau ran off to the barn to get acquainted with Mitt and Payze, grant them friendship. Later, Rube indicated that Hans occupy his bedroom where there was a saddle blanket at the foot of his bed.

But in spite of his newly acquired guardians, Rube didn't rest or sleep that night. In the morning he could hardly move. He was tentatively applying a clean dressing to his chest wound, when Mitt and Payze walked into the house. Mitt sucked air through his teeth, shook his head.

'That ain't too handsome. Reckon you need to see a doctor,' he said. 'You got a buggy or a wagon out there somewhere?'

'If I *do* decide to see some town sawbones, I'll

make it on the roan.' Toughing it out, Rube buttoned up his shirt. 'It's sore an' stiff, just like a bullet scrape should be.'

Mitt and Payze shared a meaningful look, thought better of voicing further concern.

'Anyways, I don't much like the idea o' leavin' you two here alone,' Rube added.

Mitt smiled. 'We'll be safe enough. It's you the sheepmen want,' the cowboy warned, good-humouredly. 'Won't do 'em no good to harm Payze or me. If they think otherwise, one of us'll get back to Red Iron.'

The tight soreness in Rube's chest didn't ease off as he hoped it would. After some breakfast, he even felt worse, broke into the sweat of a mounting fever. He conceded the need to see a doctor, gritted his teeth while saddling the roan.

Once over the north creek, he took the stock trail that ran around Amis Kalfs Snakehead ranch. He held the mare to a lope for fear of falling from the saddle, so it was close to sundown when he saw the twin water towers of Coolidge ahead of him. He put the roan into the stable, then took a room at the town's boarding-house. It was drawing full dark, when he asked where he'd find the doctor.

Frank Statton MD, rolled the end of a cigar around his mouth. 'If you'd got yourself a little closer, maybe he'da shot your breast bone out,' he observed drily. He swabbed, dusted some pink powder to Rube's

82

chest wound and applied a fresh dressing. 'You don't look like the kind o' feller who'll rest up, but I'm prescribin' it, all the same,' he advised. 'Do as you please, an' the sepsis'll take hold, an' that ain't a good diagnosis.' He handed over some small packets of powder. 'Find yourself a bed, an' take two o' these.'

Rube couldn't do much else, other than go along with the doctor's advice. He felt sick and his head was throbbing. Back in his room, he swallowed the powders and lay down fully dressed. He doused the bedside lamp, and ten minutes later drifted into an exhausted sleep.

The next day was well along when he awoke. He had a cautious stretch, and washed, noticed a low reassuring growl from his stomach. Descending the stairs, he crossed the small lobby and went out on to the sidewalk. The street was thronged with oxen, horses and mules, settlers' wagons being loaded with supplies. He thought he'd look for a diner and turned down the street, walked past the mercantile store and into Louis Hark.

The newspaper publisher hesitated, before smiling a greeting. 'D'you remember me, Louis Hark? he asked. 'We met in Cuffy Deke's, the day you set down here. I been hopin' to see you again. Do you mind comin' back to the office for a few minutes.'

Rube did remember him, but it was mainly because of Hark's daughter that he agreed to walk on to the office of the *Coolidge Broadcast*.

Inside the glass-panelled building, Hark stopped beside the cluttered desk where his daughter was checking copy.

'This is my daughter Etta,' he said.

'Have we met?' Etta asked, smiling uncertainly.

Rube could have said they'd spoken outside of the saloon, but didn't. 'I think I would have remembered, miss,' he offered, as a more useful response.

'I remember you sayin' your name was Rube Cassidy,' Hark said, while he checked the tip of a new pencil. 'But now it's proven to be Rube Bird, an' you're the beneficiary o' Wild Bird.'

'Is that a question, or what?' Rube asked of him.

'Arkin' for corroboration's my way of askin' a question, I guess. Dow Lineman's a friend o' mine. He knows I make my livin' by news. So I also heard the sheep got pretty close to your land.'

'Well, *there's* your front-page story,' Rube answered, hoping it tied up the matter.

But Hark wanted a lot more than that. 'There's a story behind you, Mr Bird. So why don't we talk about it for a while?' he suggested. 'You're law abidin' an' I am too. I'm also considerin' the settlers along Ten Mile Creek. They ain't got much of a voice from out there, an' any range war will ruin 'em . . . wipe 'em out. So maybe my words will help. The pen up against the sword an' all that.'

For a moment, Rube pondered on Hark's rhetoric. 'Well, there ain't a great deal to tell,' he said, not knowing for certain what manner of story was wanted. 'I remember when we were kids, our ma an' pa took up sections in the valley. Then Pa bought some surplus railroad land, an' a couple o' vacated claims. He wanted everything between the north an' south creeks . . . a land where we'd be safe.'

Hark felt the sting of bitterness in Rube's voice. He nodded and licked the end of his pencil. 'Please go on,' he said, continuing with his notes.

'My ma died o' smallpox. We buried her on the ranch. The Laggers sheep outfit moved into the Peaks south an' west of us. Trouble started right off, right from when Pa refused to sell up. Our cattle were raided. Some were killed, the rest, run off. Laggers used the sheep then, ran 'em across the creek, straight on to Wild Bird. We held 'em though, a heap never made it back out o' the valley. They'll still be there . . . the original bone yard.'

Rube nodded his thanks to Etta, who placed a mug of coffee in front of him.

'Laggers was burned up. He grabbed what men he could, an' came back. Pa packed off me an' my brother . . . sent us to hide in the willows along the north creek. But my brother rode back, an' they killed him too.'

Hark took another pencil from a pot on the desk. 'You were on your own then?' he asked, bluntly.

'Yeah, I was on my own. There was nothin' else left. Not even a goddamn rooster. I got help from a farmer who told me he was goin' to move on. He set up the headstones, then later, brought me out in his

85

wagon. I think he'd been a long-time friend o' my parents.'

'You must have had some money?' Hark pressed, with more professional attention.

'Yeah, there was a family cache. Ma always said it was for if disaster struck . . . would get us all back east. It was enough for a year's schoolin' an' keepin' the taxes paid. The next year, I got work up north, eventually made it to the Ansel Tribune ranch. Over the years, I got to be ramrod an' acquired some stock. I guess you an' your contributors' been in on the rest o' the story, Mr Hark.'

The newspaperman made a wry smile. 'There's myths an' there's facts, Mr Bird. I do need some colour for next week's issue.'

'Tall tales, you mean. Well, I'm sorry to disappoint you, Mr Hark, but that's all I've got. I ain't no Ned Buntline,' Rube insisted. He was going to say he'd been shot, but in the circumstances thought better of it. 'I got hurt a bit, up at the creek. That's what I'm doin' here in town . . . seein' the doc. Now, if you'll excuse me, I'm hungry . . . need me some breakfast.'

Hark was still not going to be put off. He went off again with his persuasive talk, but Etta saved him from Rube's growing ire, by interrupting.

'Mr Bird's right, Pa,' she said firmly. 'An' you know better than to keep a man from his food.' She paused, smiled supportively at Rube. 'Would you mind if I came with you? It seems like days ago that I had *my* breakfast.'

86

'No, Miss Etta, be my guest.' Rube hoped there was an alternative to the buffalo doin's he'd had in mind. He turned to Hark. 'I've been Rube Cassidy for a good many years, an' the name's kind o' stuck. For now, I'd like to leave it that way, if you don't mind,' he said.

14

LEGAL WRANGLE

There was an eating place not far along from the newspaper offices, and Etta suggested that they take a seat there. From a list of meals that leaned towards beef, Rube went for stew.

Etta had her coffee, didn't say much until she saw Rube eyeing the dark gravy that remained on his plate.

'Well, what do you normally do?' she asked with a smile.

Rube shrugged, soaked the remains of a sour-dough wedge.

'Wild Bird must be a fine spead,' Etta remarked, to get a conversation going.

Rube agreed. Then described Wild Bird and what it meant to him, for a few minutes surprised himself with an almost lyrical depiction.

'I'd like to see it some day,' Etta responded, as they stepped back out on to the sidewalk.

'Yeah, then you can tell me somethin' about you,' Rube said, looking wholly pleased.

Hark wasn't in the office when they returned. Rube hung up his hat, and Etta spread a recent, previous issue of the *Broadcast* across a copy desk. Almost the whole of the front page was devoted to news of the sheep–cattle war. Much of it was speculation, but there was no doubt of Hark's pathway as he hammered on about the plight of blameless settlers along Ten Mile Creek; the inevitability of innocents suffering the worst and most.

Rube placed a finger on the last line. 'Yeah, ain't that the guts of it,' he muttered. Then, the nerve in the corner of his eye twitched. He realized that if the settlers did suffer, it would mean sheepmen were actually moving back on to Wild Bird; that he, himself, had been removed.

Etta saw that Rube was bothered, was about to ask about it, when the bell over the door rang. Her father and Digby Wonnok entered the office.

The sheriff was carrying a scattergun which he laid along the coat hooks inside the door. He nodded recognition at Rube. 'How you doin'?' he said. 'I heard about your meetin' with Fortine an' Wist. They're back in Garden City now. I caught the mail stage, thought I'd give the situation the legal eye, so to speak. If it gets any worse, I'll be recommendin' some support for Sewett.'

'We got some news regardin' *your* property . . .
Wild Bird,' Hark said. 'There's nothin' for Quorrel
and Winder to answer to, apparently.'

Wonnock nodded. 'That's right. Quorrel's lawyer
claimed they were claimin' rights of unworked land.
It's a hard one to prove, though. Winder suggested
they might sue for bein' hit, out east o' the Peaks.'

'Makes you wonder what side the law's on,' Hark
said scathingly.

'The law's the law,' Wonnock chuckled gruffly and
turned to Rube. 'I'd like a private word,' he said, and
walked to the back of the office. He stepped into a
small composing-room, out of Etta and her father's
sight.

'Has it occurred to you, that you're some sort o'
lodestone here?' he asked.

'You must have a biblical streak runnin' through
you, Sheriff,' Rube retorted, after a moment's hesita-
tion. 'You suggestin' I turn a cheek, my back, even?'

Wonnok shook his head good-naturedly. 'Turn
whatever you like, you'll still be in the sheepmen's
way. I'm mentionin' it, 'cause I want you to stay alive.
You know as well as me, them sheep ain't goin' to stay
south o' the creek for long.'

Rube leaned in close to the sheriff. 'If you want me
or anyone else to stay alive, give 'em the attention
your goddamn law's been heapin' on Quorrel an
Winder. I'm only lookin' out for what's mine. Who
are you supportin' here?'

'You. An' long term. Have you thought o' what

90

happens if you get yourself laid out? What becomes o' Wild Bird?' Wonnock asked.

'The same as if I *don't*, it sounds like,' Rube said, quick and without thinking.

'O' course, if you had someone to leave it to, no sheep would ever get to leave its sign on the land. That's a certainty, an' goes for the likes o' Quorrel too. This has always been cow country. You can make sure it stays that way.'

Rube turned around and looked through to the office. He saw that Hark and Etta were doing a poor job of not listening, and he allowed them a spare smile. 'Makes it pretty dumb shootin' me out o' the saddle as well,' he answered Wonnok. 'Is one o' them self-writ wills, fair for a court?'

'Yeah. In Kansas they are.'

'In that case, I'll get one penned,' Rube said. 'Thank you, Sheriff.'

Wonnok's face worked with incredulity as he followed Rube back to Hark's writing-desk. Rube had already noticed the ink pots, paper and pens. He moved aside the news sheet, sat down and smoothed a sheet of foolscap. Shielding his writing with one arm, he wrote the date, thoughtfully filled nearly half of one page. Five minutes later he doubled over the part he'd written, signed beneath it and took it to the sheriff who was talking with Hark and Etta.

'This is the will. It'll need a witness to my signature here,' he pointed out.

Wonnok took the pen from Rube, wrote his full name alongside Rube's. 'Needs another,' he said, and handed the paper to Etta.

'Ahh, let your pa do that,' Rube intercepted. 'You know, with him bein' the editor an' all. Gives such a thing a kind o' weight. Sorry, Miss Etta,' he added, with some discomfort.

'That's all right,' she chirped up. 'I was just thinking, how much trouble could be avoided if *everyone wrote a will.*'

'Could be responsible for some early deaths, too,' Wonnok rumbled.

Hark opened a drawer of his desk, gave Rube an envelope. 'Where you goin' to keep it?' he asked.

'I was *hopin'* you could look after it. You'd be the best person, in case of it havin' to be opened.'

Hark nodded and took back the envelope, wrote something in the top corner. Then he looked up, his face showing that he'd just thought of something else. 'Spoke to the doc, earlier,' he said, looking at Rube. 'He said he'd given you something that would bring a mule to its knees. Ain't it workin'?'

'Yeah, it worked. But recently, I been helpin' to sell some news sheets.' As he spoke, Rube was aware though, that his fever was returning.

'An' we're real appreciative,' Hark replied with a smile. 'But thinkin' about it, why not take advantage o' the town bein' quiet? For as long as it lasts, do what everyone else does.'

'An' what would that be?' Rube wondered.

'Well, I don't rightly know the detail, but you could get your head down for a bit. You look as though you could use some sleep.'

Involuntarily, Rube yawned at the thought. He realized that the sheriff had probably been speculating on what he'd been seeing the doctor for. But that was nothing more than Rube's business. He was also concerned about Mitt and Payze getting jumpy with him being gone so long. 'Yeah,' he said, slow and thoughtful, 'that's good advice. An' I guess I'm just about finished here.'

Rube thanked Hark and the sheriff, took his hat from Etta. He made his way out of the offices, started along the sidewalk towards the boarding-house.

15

NO SURRENDER

As he walked in the sharp, street-side shadows, Rube heard movement from an alleyway that emerged beside Cuffs' Deke's. Then someone spoke and he stopped, took a sideways step into the street.

It was two of Rush Orlick's partners who had been waiting for him. First off, Rube recognized the cavalrymen's gunbelts, then the men's faces that were no meaner or cleaner than the last time he'd seen them.

'I said you'd regret not shootin' us, mister,' the taller of the two men threatened, stepping onto the sidewalk proper.

Rube recalled it was the one who went by the name of Maggs. 'Quorrel snaps his fingers, an' you jump. Is that it?' he said brusquely.

Maggs shook his head. 'This is purely personal. It's between me, Trove an' you,' he scowled.

And Rube believed it. What happened next, would be regardless of anyone else's orders. These two were intent on revenge because of Rube sending them barefoot across open rangeland.

Maggs quickly stepped forward as Trove moved around behind Rube.

'The walk *you're* goin' on's a long, long trail . . . a real killer,' Maggs sneered.

Rube guessed what was coming in behind the words. He swung his body sideways, so that Maggs's rising knee hit him in the thigh. It was a hard blow, and Rube's left leg went instantly numb from the impact. Cursing, Maggs swung a fist at Rube's face. It smashed into his cheek as Rube tried to swing his head out of the way. It sent his hat flying, mashing the inside of his cheek against his teeth.

As Maggs came on, Rube staggered back. He felt Trove's arms clasp tight around his chest, the hot breath on the back of his neck.

'Goddamn gunny-sacker,' the man grunted.

Rube drew the tip of his tongue away from his teeth, expected a beating that would go way beyond the normal cow-town brawl. He swung both his legs up into the air as Maggs lashed out with another fist. The lunge pushed Trove backwards. Maggs missed, and Rube's boots caught him full and low.

Trove grunted, crumpled around his winded belly, and Rube brought his heel down viciously on the top of his foot. There was a short gasp of pain, and Rube stamped again, even harder. He felt the crunch of foot bones and, locking the fingers of his hands, fetched his arms up. The bear hug was broken, and Rube broke free of Trove's arms and the crushing hurt. He turned quickly, piled a short, savage blow into the man's middle.

Then he stepped forward and punched him full-fisted in the mouth. The teeth moved, and Trove's head crashed back as far as the corner post of the saloon.

But now Maggs was on his feet, and charging back at Rube. His arms were windmilling and his face was contorted with uncontrolled rage. His momentum carried him across Rube's dropped shoulder and he pitched headlong into the slumped body of his partner.

Rube stepped back as Maggs landed in a mash of arms and legs. 'I'm supposed to be convalescin',' he growled, suddenly feeling the renewed pain in his chest.

For the second time, and pulling at the flap of his holster, Maggs got unsteadily to his feet. 'Do that when you're dead,' he gasped, drawing a Colt.

Maggs was nowhere near fast enough though, and Rube was in. He lashed the knuckles of his right hand sideways, into Maggs' wrist, fast back again into the man's grimy face. As the nose blood spurted, Rube stepped away, cursed his misfortune, Coolidge and sheepmen. Then he heard the thump of feet on the sidewalk behind him, and he turned, swore again.

'I ain't in shape for any more goddamn fist fightin',' he wheezed, and took some short deep breaths.

Sheriff Wonnok had the scattergun in his right hand, was swinging up the barrels as he strode towards the fight. 'I'll take him, son. Leave your gun be,' he called to Rube.

Maggs, his face a mask of slimy blood, was getting to his feet, raising his Colt for another go at Rube. He'd got the hammer dragged fully back, and his finger was tightening on the trigger when Rube threw himself from the sidewalk.

The two shots were fired almost simultaneously, but the blast from Wonnok's gun overwhelmed the sound of Maggs' Colt. Without breaking stride, the sheriff was hauling back for the next barrel.

Maggs was in mid air, hands clawing for his Colt that was already lying in the dirt of the street. There was an ominous pool of blood spread across his side and chest as he thudded into the ground. He managed to get to his knees, as his eyes clouded. A crushed lip curled back over jagged teeth, and he spat a final hex at Rube. Then he pitched forward and died.

Wonnok lowered his scattergun. 'He wouldn'ta surrendered,' he gritted.

'No. Wouldn't've even taken a warnin'. Seems that sheepmen prefer to die,' Rube sided with the county sheriff.

Maggs's partner was on all fours, crawling by the

low weather-boarding of Cuffy Deke's. He stopped, raised his hands defensively around his darkly bruised head.

Wonnok snarled at him, 'Either way, you're finished, mister. I don't recommend you carry on the fight.'

Trove tried to get up. He howled in distress, then fell sideways as the foot cracked by Rube's boot heel, gave way.

'I wanna doctor,' were his last words, before his head fell forward.

'My heart's bleedin' for you,' Rube said. He looked back along the street, saw Etta Hark, before staggering into a dizzy blackness.

16

HEADLINE NEWS

The extra physic that Doc Statton had administered had done its work well. Rube opened his eyes, looked around him, then raised himself on an elbow. He had some tightness, but little pain. He reckoned that a brace of stiff whiskeys, then plenty of strong coffee, was the next stage of his healing, and he said so.

'An' how'd you propose to get from here to Cuffy Deke's with no pants,' Wonnok observed. I'd have to arrest you.'

Rube had a look under the sheets. 'On what charge?' he asked idly.

'How about, no visible means o' support,' the sheriff quipped, and the men laughed.

Louis Hark was looking down into the street from the window of the boarding-house. 'Those sheepmen ain't goin' to roll over,' he said, ominously. 'Not now.

This is the start of another war, *not* sabre rattlin', Sheriff.'

'It was nothin' more'n street cleanin',' Wonnok returned dismissively.

Hark shook his head discontentedly. 'Well, the *Broadcast* has got itself a print run,' he said, and waved a hand at Rube as he left the room.

'An' I'm visitin' the jailhouse,' Statton said. 'Sewett's got himself someone down there, who's sufferin' from bad feet.'

'How is he?' Etta asked, as soon as Hark returned to the office. 'They were Greasy Quorrel's men, weren't they?'

'Yeah,' her father said irately. 'Names are Maggs an' Trove. Maggs is dead, 'cause Wonnok shot him. Cassidy ain't hurt bad. The does filled him with laudanum or some such.'

Hark sat down at his desk, pulled the foolscap and started his writing. 'Get the comp in, Etta. I want him to make up an extra,' he said.

The lead story flowed fast from Hark's pen. It was a thrilling account of how two murderous thugs hid in the shadows, waiting to backshoot an innocent man, a man who was already full of painkilling medicine, a man who was making his way through the sleepy cow town to find a sickbed.

Satisfied with his hyperbole, Hark considered a headline, the new-found excitement from the townsfolk when the news-sheet hit the street.

For the rest of the day, and through a morphine-induced sleep, Rube got the rest he needed. It was well into full dark when he pulled himself up to look bleary-eyed at the lamps along the sidewalks. But the doc had administered fittingly, and he slumped down from the window, slept even more soundly throughout the night.

In the morning, Rube lifted a hand and tugged at the blind that had been pulled sometime during the early hours. He swung his legs to the floor, sat for a few minutes and marshalled his thoughts, dredged up memories of the street fight. Then he noticed his pain-killing powders were no longer on the bedside table, guessed it was Doc Statton who'd visited.

He had a cold water wash from a basin, and got himself dressed. He was buckling on his gunbelt, when there was a knock at the door.

'Yeah, come on in,' he called, rested the palm of his hand on the butt of his Colt.

Dub Sewett opened the door and walked in. 'Mornin',' he said, taking off his hat. 'From what I been hearin', we'd've got to meet again before long.'

Rube nodded. 'At this hour, I'm guessin' you're not here to tell me *that*, Marshal.'

'Er no, there's somethin' else,' Sewett said, a little uncomfortably. 'Greasy Quorrel asked me to find you. If you're well enough, he wants to talk to you. He's over at Cuffy Deke's.'

'If I'm *well* enough?' Rube almost laughed. 'That's real funny. The man's got some neck, sendin' a town marshal to do his biddin'.' Tension flowed back into Rube's body. 'Got a bushwhacker along has he?' he asked bitingly. 'I know of *one or two* who ain't dead or busted up.'

'He's alone. An' he come to town alone, too. He says he paid off all his hired hands. Maggs an' Trove were out for 'emselves, not workin' for him. I'm here, tryin' to peacemake.'

Rube turned away from Sewett. He thought he might as well go and find out what Quorrel wanted, and he wasn't likely to come to much harm at Cuffy Deke's.

'Lead on. I don't want to be the one who got in the way o' peace,' he said, tightly.

The sheepman sat at a corner table, away from the saloon's early customers. He was wearing a dark suit, no spurs. It was obvious he hadn't come to town riding a horse.

As he turned towards Rube, Sewett hesitated.

'You stay,' Rube told him. 'As an agent o' the law, I want you to hear every word.'

Quorrel gave a thin smile as the two men approached the table. 'I was wantin' this to be between you an' me,' he said, his face hardening up.

'I'm sure. But the marshal stays. I've had enough o' your private stuff,' Rube retorted.

Quorrel sucked air through his teeth, vaguely gestured at Sewett. If you're alludin' to the low-life that came after you yesterday, I only got back from

Garden City this mornin'. An' them two no longer work for me or Clete Winder. All we got now's a few herdsmen an' camp tenders.'

Rube didn't believe the man, looked around as if he'd got something else on his mind.

'I've got a proposal. Take a seat an' listen,' Quorrel continued.

'Give me one good reason why I should listen to the likes o' you?' Rube said scornfully.

Quorrel gave a small, scheming grin. 'I'll give you fifty thousand of 'em. That's a lot o' jack for the land, an' a cowpen herd. What do you say, cowboy?'

'I'm sayin', I ain't that cowboy no longer,' Rube answered back. 'Suddenly, I'm a big casino with fifty thousand dollars worth o' range land an' stock. An' what's more, I ain't in the business o' sellin' another cowman down the goddamn creek.'

Quorrel squeezed his whiskey glass, coloured up threateningly. 'I'm offerin' more than double what the place is worth, mister, an' you know it.'

Rube turned to have a closer look at the saloon's customers. He was looking for Orlick and Poole, wondered why Quorrel hadn't wanted Dub Sewett to stay.

'You got to think on a broader front, Cassidy,' Quorrel advised. 'Think what that sort o' money's really buyin'. We'll only be runnin' our sheep on to Wild Bird for winter feed. The rest o' the time, we'll be on leased land, south o' Buzzard Peaks. There'll be no eatin' of other people's grass, or other people's anythin'. Whether there's any more fightin' or not's up to you.'

Rube didn't take to Quorrel's attempt at blackmail and glared icily. He wondered whether to say he'd willed the land over. Instead, he turned his back and walked across to the bar.

The marshal was alongside him. 'A mighty hand-some offer,' he hinted cautiously.

'I'll burn it . . . blow the whole place apart, before lettin' a single goddamn sheep graze on Wild Bird.' Rube threatened. Then he remembered what Digby Wonnok had said if the situation in the valley got any worse. 'An' you'll be gettin' some support,' he added wryly.

It dawned on him now, that for the want of a different name, everything was running as it had so many years before, when the Laggers outfit moved murderously on the Bird family.

An affecting shudder ran through Rube's body. In his mind, he realized the next moves of Quorrel and Winder. Dow Lineman was right: the sheepmen never intended to quit the valley. They were back, offering a peace plan under the nose of the law. But it was a ruse, a prelude to them getting rough, the promised blood of a fight.

They'd send hired gunmen across the creeks from the north and south. Rube's small herd would be run into the Peaks to die. The Poll Durhams would prob-ably be taken to Ulysses or Johnson, sold for a night's gambling stake. If any remained, they'd be shot where they stood, their carcasses left as ruthless messages. And then, if Rube was still there, they'd make a final and deadly move on him.

'You want to know what happens next?' he asided to Sewett. 'I'm goin' to do what's best for all of us, an' put some bullets into Quorrel. All a town marshal's got to do, is close his eyes for a moment.'

Sewett swallowed hard. His facial expression fused fear and amusement as he watched Rube move away from the bar.

Rube didn't even look at Quorrel as he left the saloon. On the sidewalk, he squinted at the still rising sun and took a few deep breaths. He wasn't going to try and make it back home that day he decided.

He spent the next few hours in his room, resting up some more. It was approaching dusk when he went along to see Etta Hark. She was pleased to see him, and invited him out to the house for supper.

He left Coolidge at sun-up the next morning, took the roan into a fast clip for Wild Bird.

17

THE LET OFF

'Mr Lineman sent a rider. He wants us,' Mitt had to tell Rube the moment he rode in. 'The goddamn sheep are back. They're strung along the Peaks . . . pressin' hard against Red Iron. The boss figures they could be gettin' ready to make a move on him. We got to be there. He said you'd understand.'

'Yeah, I understand,' Rube sighed. 'So much for the neighbourly support, eh?'

'No, it ain't like that,' Payze said. 'We sent word back: Said why you'd gone to Coolidge, that you'd be needin' us.'

Rube thanked them for their watchfulness anyway, for feeding his dogs. He knew it didn't matter much whether they stayed or not. If Wild Bird was attacked wholesale, two or three of them weren't going to hold out. Sending a dozen armed sheepmen packing would have come second to being shot dead.

Mitt and Payze tied in their horse strings and set off to Red Iron. For what was left of the day, Rube gave distracted consideration to his dog pack.

Knowing he'd be away from the ranch house, Rube wanted the pinschers trained to stay around. The pups were already independent for some of the time. They had the full run of the house, the yard and open ground out to the barn. That night, at sundown, Hans accompanied him for a check around the corral and ruined outbuildings, for the most part, he was content to run at heel.

When it was well into full dark, Rube drew himself a blanket and some extra cartridges. He saddled a rimrock mare, and rode to the rising ground where his family were buried. In the bright moonlight, from beneath the beeches, he could see most of the way to the south fork of Ten Mile Creek, the sooty specks that were his small herd. Until the early hours he remained in the saddle, then he dismounted and sat wrapped in his blanket to await first light. But nothing happened. It was the following night when the riders came.

They came off the Peaks during the daylight hours, hid in the creek timber until near midnight, when the moon dropped below Springfield Ridge. A dull gunshot brought Rube to his feet, as the sound echo.ed along the creek from where two men rode at his herd.

They fired two, then three more shots, as the cattle started their run towards the shelter of the willow brakes. Rube tugged at the mare's cinch and mounted. 'About time I gave 'em hell, Pa,' he avowed.

Because of the distance from the Wild Bird ranch house, the riders thought they'd be safe for an hour or so, and moved around recklessly. They were laughing as they swung from six dead heifers to those that continued their stampede for cover.

Rube heeled his horse into a run, took it fast down the rising slope and on to the range. He swung in an arc to favour the east, where the north and south forks of the creek connected. He gained on the riders, wanted to cut them off from the crossing, trap them in the western end of his land.

The two men had stopped now. They were wondering which of the broke up groups of heifers to go for, when they heard the pounding approach of Rube's mare. Not expecting anyone from Wild Bird, they hesitated, turned in their saddles expecting a rider from the sheep camp. But, under the bright starlight, they realized the rider wasn't friendly, and it was too late.

Rube reined the mare into a tight swerve, skidded to a halt. He pulled his Winchester and went to ground, took up a kneeling position.

The men ahead of him began firing in fearful and heedless panic. But Rube was too far away for their Colts, and his first big .45 bullet took one of them in the middle of his back as he'd turned to flee. The featureless figure snapped forward, then back, windmilled lifelessly to the ground.

The man's horse sank to one side, then sprung its legs and bucked as the other rider yelled curses. The man decided to run for the sandy steeps below Springfield Ridge. It was where the bleached, sheep bones lay.

'Fittin', but you'll never make it,' Rube hissed icily.

As the man spurred his horse west, he twisted in the saddle, looked back to see if Rube was chasing.

Rube smiled coldly and took aim again, shot the man high in the right shoulder. He lowered the rifle, watched as the man clutched with one hand at the mane of his horse. Then he got to his feet, calmly shoved the rifle back into its saddle holster, and swung into the saddle. He gently heeled the mare forward. 'Needn't run. He ain't goin' far,' he murmured.

Rube kept his eyes alert as he drew close. The man had managed to recover his reins, but it was as much as he could do to stay upright. He didn't even turn to confront his foe. Rube pulled off to one side, then swung the mare in close.

'I got your bullet in me, mister,' the man croaked. 'What else you goin' to do?'

Rube drew his Winchester, leaned over and slammed its barrel hard against the man's leg. 'You been killin' my cattle . . . tryin' to shoot me dead, you scum sucker. So, I'm goin' to set fire to your ass . . . see if you smell like mutton.'

The man let out a low groan at the agony of his cracked kneecap. 'I ain't no sheepman, mister,' he

109

whined. 'I jus' gone took me some work at fightin' wages. You know how it is.'

'Yeah, tough, if you ain't got the hang of it. Any more o' your kind on my range this night?' Rube demanded.

'Nobody come, but us.'

'Who sent you?'

'Tekker Poole. He said you wouldn't have a guard out yet . . . didn't have men to cover the range.'

'Yeah, well I ain't as stupid as some. What do you know about Poole?' Rube asked.

'Nothin' much. We weren't told nothin' about nobody.'

Rube switched the barrel of the rifle threateningly. 'I'd make somethin' up, if I was you,' he threatened.

'He's been heard to say he wants you under his feet.'

Rube's eyes narrowed. 'Where's he come from?' The man shook his head miserably. 'Somewhere north o' here, I think.'

Rube guessed the man didn't have much more to offer. 'North, you say? I'm reckonin' that Poole an' me must've had a run-in before. Maybe, he's got more'n the edge o' memory.'

The man gave a painful, almost inaudible grunt. 'Don't know . . . don't care. If you ain't goin' to finish me off, let me ride,' he risked.

'You think you can make the State line without stoppin . . . without fallin'?' Rube goaded.

'I'll die tryin'.'

'That you might. If you do make it, I'd think about keepin' store for a livin',' Rube suggested. He moved the mare back a few steps, indicated the way north with the tip of his rifle. He speculated that if, when he got to the ridge, the man folded trail to forewarn the sheepmen, it would be late the next day before they got back.

Rube watched the man and his horse walk away, until they vanished into the darkness. Then he rode back to where he'd shot the other man, gathered the horse that hadn't wandered far. Hurting and sweating, he managed to rope the man and drag his body up and over the horse's back. He hog-tied the man's feet beneath the horse's belly and punched the animal's thigh, sent it trotting towards the north creek crossing. He wanted the body off his Wild Bird range, wanted it back in Coolidge.

18

THE SELF-DEFENCE

At the newspaper office, Dub Sewett walked in from the blistering heat of mid-afternoon. He removed his hat, and wiped a bandanna across the top of his forehead. Louis Hark greeted him, and Etta smiled from where she was sitting at her father's desk, copy-writing.

'Reckon it's hotter'n yesterday,' the marshal suggested.

'Yeah, in more'n one way,' Hark returned. 'Any more news on the stiff?'

'Not yet. There's a whole bunch o' sheepmen in town, an' they know nothin' either.'

'Now why don't that surprise me?' Hark said, making a wry smile.

'The feller who brought him in, still maintains it was Rube Cassidy who bushwhacked 'em.'

Etta, shook her head sadly. 'Well, that surprises *me*,' she said, and looked to her father.

'What are the sheepmen doin' in town?' Hark asked Sewett.

'Right now they're loadin' up with supplies.'

'You goin' to do anythin' about it?'

Sewett gave Hark a quizzical look. 'Buyin' peas an' hog meat from Jammer Miley's is lawful enough,' he said. 'You think there's a problem, Louis?'

'Yep. An' I'd say in about ten minutes. I just seen Peeler an' Walt with their boys. Looked to me like they were headed straight for trouble.'

'I saw 'em too, an' warned 'em off,' Sewett said. 'I don't reckon there'll be much of a story there.'

But both men had got it wrong. They ran from the building as the first blast of gunfire erupted from along the street.

A bunch of Lone-Tree men ran from the doors of the Running Steer. They were shooting back into the building as they jumped to the street.

'Goddamn Bose waddies,' Sewett swore, as he started off along the sidewalk.

Hark was close behind as the marshal pushed his way through the batwings. With their backs to the bar, stood Walt and Peeler Bose. To their left, two more of their ranch hands were watching a corner table.

Clete Winder and Tekker Poole were sitting opposite their own hired men, one of whom had taken a shot across the flesh of his neck. Another man

113

glanced warily at the marshal, before continuing to souse his colleague's bloody wound with whiskey.

Sewett halted in the centre of the floor, Hark backed up to the bar to assess the story.

'Now I can see why we call it "neck oil",' Sewett rasped. 'But you've wasted enough. If you can walk, get out . . . all o' you,' he commanded.

Not one of the men moved, and Sewett turned his attention to Peeler Bose.

'I just got through tellin' you not to cause any trouble, Peeler. What the hell is it with you cow men?'

'You stay out o' this, Dub. Usin' language they understand, we're tellin' these lamb lickers they don't belong. Told 'em we got ourselves some segregation.'

'There's ground muck that's higher up the social scale than some as drink here, Peeler, an' you know it. How did this start?'

'What the hell difference does that make?' Winder demanded.

'We told 'em to leave. This one here went for his gun,' Walt said indicating the man he'd shot. That makes it self-defence, Marshal.'

'An' your boys that were shootin' the place up; who or what the hell were they defendin'?' Sewett enquired testily.

'They just got a tad excited, Marshal, that's all.'

Sewett took a deep breath and momentarily closed his eyes. 'Your wagon must be about loaded,' he told

114

Winder. 'Just get out o' town before anythin' else happens.' With his hand on his Colt, the marshal suggested the sheepmen get out of their chairs and follow him.

The men assembled on the sidewalk outside of the saloon, watched amazed as a heavily loaded wagon raced along the street towards them. The driving seat was empty, but holding the reins of the mule team, a Lone Tree cowboy rode alongside.

'What the hell. . . !' was just about all the men's reactions as the rider dragged the team to a straight line.

The big wagon swayed drunkenly, the mules bog-eyed with panic. Some of the trace chains had been unhooked, and laden with food supplies, the whole outfit was headed for a break up. A mixed bunch of riders from the valley ranches chased-up close behind. They were hollering, waving their hats with one hand, firing off their Colts in the other.

'They musta loco'd my mules to make 'em run like that,' Winder rasped, while the Bose brothers shrugged insolently.

The dust billowed from beneath the wheels, almost hid the wagon as it careered to the very edge of town. Then the cowboy let the team free and, snapping the remaining traces, the mules ran on wildly. The wagon swerved and hit the base of one of the water towers, with a grinding of wood and iron, twisted over onto its side. Through the choking alkali clouds, most of the sheepmen's provisions were

115

strewed pathetically across the hard-packed dirt.

Sewett stepped down from the sidewalk. 'The fun's over,' he yelled. 'Peeler, you an' Walt stand aside. The first of your men to pull a gun, gets all found for a week.'

Peeler Bose considered a response as he looked to his brother, then nodded his observance. 'You boys behave, you hear,' he called out reluctantly. 'Let 'em go. I doubt we'll be bothered again.'

The sheepmen who'd been watching, stepped anxiously from various buildings along the street. Winder and Poole strolled grudgingly to where all the horses were hitched. The injured man threw a mean look back at Walt, but he saw the marshal was watching him and thought better of going for his gun.

Sewett turned tautly, as one of Jammer Miley's store clerks came running up.

'Marshal, they ain't paid,' the man flustered.

'Yeah, ain't life a bitch,' Sewett drawled irritatedly. 'You go tell Jammer, that if he wants payment, Clete Winder ain't left town yet. That goes for the goods too, if you don't mind a mouthful o' grit. Personally, I'd think about chalkin' it up.'

Diagonally, across the street, Winder kicked his horse into movement. What he had in mind came quick, and it wasn't what Marshal Sewett was expecting. Having already pulled his Colt on the blind side, Winder twisted in the saddle, fired off three quick shots at the group of men still standing outside of the saloon.

Walt Bose's Colt had cleared leather before Winder had fired his first shot. But Peeler made a grab for his brother's wrist. By the time the bullets had crashed into the front of the Running Steer, all the sheepmen were away, heads down, headed for out of town and the open range.

Sewett was standing his ground, had hardly moved. His mind raced at the implications of what had just happened, what it would mean. The sheepmen had been prevented from obtaining their much-needed supplies. That meant they'd be making an alternative arrangement. Somewhere and sometime soon, someone was going to pay. From where Sewett stood, it looked like Louis Hark could be right about the settlers along Ten Mile Creek.

In the meantime, he had a feeling there'd be something on a circular or dodger sent out from the county seat. There invariably was on a man who came to town hog-tied to his horse and dead.

19

A WANTED MAN

The pinschers were now barking in unison as the threat got closer, as the lone rider emerged from the creekside timber, and headed directly for the ranch.

Cradling the rifle, Rube took a step on to the belt of ground that had been cleared to the home pasture. 'Hans, Frau!' he shouted, and the dogs stopped their warning noises. They were still guarded, but walked at heel, as Rube walked out to meet Etta Hark. Rube raised his hand in greeting. 'Like me, they ain't too sure yet what breeds are friendly,' he called out, as she drew close.

'I said, I'd come visit, didn't I?' Etta replied. 'Yeah, but I didn't know you meant it. Just to be neighbourly like.'

'Oh, I meant it. It's sooner, because there's something else, Rube.'

'What else?'

'Dub Sewett's got a warrant for your arrest.'

'My arrest! What for? Who from?'

'The man who brought in the body of the man you're supposed to have murdered.'

'Ah, him . . . the lucky one,' Rube said, reaching out to take hold of the bay's cheek strap. 'Had a bullet wound, did he? High in the shoulder? Probably needed some help in gettin' off his horse.'

'Yes, that's right, he did . . . all those things. Was that your doing, Rube?'

'Yeah. But only after the both of 'em killed my cattle. What was his story?'

'He said they were looking for farm work. He swore someone ambushed them south of Ten Mile Creek.'

Rube felt the tightness of anger churn his insides. The man he'd let ride for the State line had turned back to Quorrel and Winder, after all. If the men hadn't any known links with the sheepmen, they'd have easily fronted-up as innocent, wandering cowpunchers. He ground his teeth. 'I learned somethin' about sheepmen: treat 'em merciful, an' them or theirs'll strike you back.'

Etta saw the turmoil in Rube's face. 'I'm sorry,' she said. 'I told Pa I didn't believe it.'

'Well, that's somethin',' he replied. 'At least you spotted I ain't a natural born killer. Do you want to

119

see the ranch? There'll be time to eat before you return,' he suggested diffidently. 'I ain't that far off bein' civilized, either.'

'I knew that, as well,' Etta said, with an agreeable smile as she climbed down from her horse. She'd seen the pups as they tumbled from around the corner of the corral fence. She knelt beside them, drew back her hand when they both yipped and gnashed their teeth.

'They ain't for pettin',' Rube explained shortly. 'Bein' friendly'll give 'em the wrong idea.'

Etta stood back. She eyed the young pinschers apprehensively while Rube collected his roan and walked it back to the barn to saddle up. A little later, Rube led the way through the home pasture, up the rising grassy trail, north of the ranch house.

'It's pretty obvious where this is,' he said, a half-hour later, where they stopped beneath the shady overhang of the blue beeches.

'Yes,' she said, looking down at the gravestones of Rube's family.

'It ain't the highest point, but you can see the span o' the land ... the best grazin' anyways.' Rube pointed to the east, along the creekside willow. 'An' you can just make out the carcasses o' my dead heifers,' he added harshly. 'Them that died with cold, gunny bullets in 'em.'

Silently now, Rube swung his horse south, down towards the creek. After a reflective moment, Etta followed.

'Do you think there's a way out of this . . . this mess?' she asked, as they approached the creekside willows.

'There sure as hell is, young lady,' Tekker Poole grated, as he moved his horse from the cover of the timber.

Rube cursed. Out of the corner of an eye, he saw Poole, and the two riders close behind him. This time, he knew he'd die unless he acted fast. Poole and him had one thing in common: neither of them were up for another chance.

As the thought crossed Rube's mind, he was already moving. He leaped from the saddle towards Etta. He yelled, and punched a fist into the bay's rump, wanted to jump them away from where he knew the bullets would come. Then he went to ground, turned on to his back and pulled his Colt. The bullets were already erupting the ground beside him as he shot one of the men behind Poole. The man gurgled bloodily, was clawing at his throat as he fell from the saddle. The riderless horse, screamed its terror. Surrounded by the crash of guns, it lashed out its forelegs at the rear of Poole's horse.

With Poole now trying to gain control of his mount, Rube couldn't find him with a bullet. The man realized that Rube's fury was already making up for any disadvantage. The cries of his colleague writhing on the ground panicked him into turning his horse back towards the creek.

Rube heard Etta's choking cry as he fired off more offensive rounds, but there was no time to look out for her. He curled up and started to reload his Colt, jerked involuntarily as bullets got closer to his body. Using his elbows, he dragged himself to where earth runnels met the broken ground of the creek timber. Poole's second back-up rider was bearing down on him, but it was Poole that Rube wanted. He fired into the willows, but knew he was wasting bullets. Poole would be kicking his horse along the creek, heading towards the sandy steeps of Springfield Ridge.

The back-up rider had halted his run, was suddenly shooting wildly. He was fearful of Rube, and looked for Poole, called for his help. Rube hit him high in the leg, and he swayed in the saddle. His horse felt the loss of control and went into a frightened gallop, away from the sound of the guns.

Rube went into a crouching run. He reached the creek, pressed his back against the bend of a willow. A bullet chewed into the silvery bark alongside his head and he ducked. The man on the ground was mortally wounded though, and had fired his last shot. He died before taking a second bullet from Rube.

Rube fired a bullet along the creek in frustration, another into the air as a measure of his hardiness. Then he stepped calmly into the open, caught sight of a darkly dressed figure who'd quickly moved in and out of the timber a long ways to the west. He loaded up again, looked doggedly around him, and pushed the Colt back into its holster.

20

FREE AGAIN

Rube met Etta with an unsmiling look as she approached. Her face was drained of colour, and she was carrying the reins of his horse.

'That should slow 'em down some,' he said drily. 'No more trouble until the next time.' He ignored the body on the ground, waved a hand at the loose horse to run it off.

'Who were they?' Etta asked quietly.

'A man named Tekker Poole. He had two of his pack with him. But I think he's been here before. It was a long time past, and he was with the Laggers' sheep outfit, then.'

'He was one of the people who murdered your family?'

Rube nodded sharply. 'Yeah, but they ain' *people*, Etta. They're sheepmen, an' there's a big difference.

I'm thinkin' Poole's the reason Quorrel and Winder tried to muscle in on Wild Bird. I reckon he'd convinced 'em they could get in here, despite the consequences.'

Etta handed Rube his reins. 'That makes some sort of sense . . . maybe. It's reminded me what else I had to tell you. Some of those sheepmen raided a farm along the creek . . . took some food supplies and a horse. There's going to be a farmers' meeting tonight. Pa advised them to get organized for their own protection.'

Rube nodded as he considered what Etta had said. 'You've had a busy day, young lady. Stayed too long. You'll be leavin' right away, I guess.'

'I'm not going anywhere. Not while there's the likelihood of running into those men. I'm staying over if it's all right with you, get an early start in the morning.'

Rube smiled and nodded slowly. He was glad Etta had made the suggestion, rather than him. 'I got me a bakin' oven. Maybe I can make you that meal I spoke of earlier,' he suggested. 'How about canned peach pie?'

'On its own?'

'No, with gravy,' he laughed, climbing into the saddle. 'Let's go.'

Immediately they'd eaten, Rube made coffee and called for Hans. 'I haven't slept inside the house too much recently. I stay awake most nights, sleep in the daytime. There'll be no more fightin'. Nevertheless,

I'll take this rascal, have a scout around . . . make sure.'

As Rube hesitated in the doorway, Etta left the table and stepped up to him. She stood very close and lifted her face. Rube held her shoulders, gave her a short, but concentrated kiss. Then he smiled, and grabbed his rifle, walked into the starlit night. With the way things were stacking up, there was no way he was going to take a ride around his ranch. He lay down among the grain sacks, slept with the warmth of Hans alongside him.

He was awake before the sun broke from the distant Red Hills. Etta had already made warm scones, coffee on top of the stove. After the early breakfast he saddled their horses and accompanied her to the crossing at the north fork of Ten Mile Creek.

'At the first sign o' trouble, take your hat off. Let 'em see you're just a slip of a girl,' he advised.

'What do I do at the second sign?' she asked, with a warm smile.

Ase Perry was sitting on the planked stoop, waiting, when Rube got back.

'You had any *other* visitors lately?' he asked, getting to his feet, extending his big hand in greeting.

Rube realized that Perry must have seen him with Etta, as he rode from the timber along the south creek. 'What do you mean?' he answered, uneasy at the farmer's question.

'Hah, you obviously ain't heard. The sheep–cattle war's over. It's ended.'

Rube stopped from turning the key in the door lock, turned slowly to look at Perry. 'The sheepmen have trailed through the Peaks, gone south,' Perry continued. 'They reckon there's enough land down there for summer an' winter grazin'. That's the word from Garden City. Digby Wonnok's confirmed it.'

'An' I'm Little Bo Peep,' Rube mumbled. He listened with deep scepticism, as Perry told him that the sheriff had been in Coolidge the day before. He'd been telling all who'd listen that the sheepmen were giving up their land push, Wild Bird included.

'Come in, why don't you. Got some coffee, should still be hot.' Rube said distractedly. Perry stayed talking for fifteen minutes. He didn't mention that there was a warrant of any kind out for Rube, and Rube didn't ask.

When the farmer had gone, Rube did some thinking. He couldn't believe the sheepmen had quit. It wasn't their way. What they wanted, they took, or died trying. But if it was the truth, there was something else. Like the personal vengeance of Tekker Poole. Yeah, that was more likely to be it. There would be no more waiting though. He'd get in first, take the fight to them once and for all.

Rube went to the barn and saddled up the roan, packed two boxes of .45 cartridges into the saddle-bags.

*

127

It was a sharp, crystal clear night when Rube nudged his horse along Coolidge's main street. He intended to be very careful, until he found out what the law intended to do about serving the warrant.

The door to the newspaper offices was open, and Rube tied the roan to the hitching rail outside. He stepped up onto the sidewalk, could see there was no sign of Etta, just Louis Hark working at his desk. He stepped through the door, and Hark turned.

'Good evenin',' the man said. 'You must've heard the war's over.'

'Yeah,' Rube said. 'I did hear somethin' o' the sort. It ain't the sort o' thing you take as gospel though, is it?'

Hark jabbed his ink pen back in its pot. 'Oh, it's over all right. It's got to be. Quorrel and Winder have pulled their sheep to the Buzzard foothills.'

'I'm guessin' there was some cattlemen out wavin' 'em goodbye,' Rube smiled his derision. 'You know, the warm, kindly types. Amis Kalf. Peeler Bose an' his brother.' Hark quickly nodded his agreement. 'I organized ... no, suggested, that the farmers get 'emselves armed ... put up a front, anyways. They won't exactly be doin' the cattlemen any harm.' But Hark could see that Rube wasn't too confident or hopeful. 'You think that's pissin' in the wind?'

'Yeah, somethin' like that. I think Tekker Poole's convinced Quorrel and Winder they can push up through the creeks ... take in Wild Bird as they go. That's why I'm in town,' Rube responded grimly.

128

'Etta told me you got caught up,' Hark said, sensing the ominous tenor in Rube's voice. 'But you'da guessed that.'

'I thought she'd probably tell you, yeah. She also said there was a murder warrant out for me.'

Hark shook his head slowly, rubbed his eyes. 'That one's goin' to be hard travellin'. Sewett found out the man's wanted in Richfield *an*' Johnson. Bank robbin' ain't one o' the accepted credentials.'

'Where's that leave me then?'

'Free again, I suppose,' Hark said, getting to his feet. 'But I'll make sure. Why don't you go over to the house an' see that daughter o' mine. I'll meet you back here in an hour.'

When Rube had gone, Hark quickly tidied up his desk. Then he grabbed his hat and coat, locked the door of the office and strolled along to Cuffy Deke's to find the town marshal.

21

GONE MISSING

Rube knew there was only one person that Hark could have asked about the warrant, and he went to find him.

Dub Sewett was in the saloon. He was at the bar, talking with some of the more prominent cattlemen.

Rube nodded at the group. 'Have you seen Mr Hark?' he asked of the marshal.

'Yep, I seen him. An' now he's gone home.'

'No he ain't,' Rube said. 'The place is in darkness. Curious, 'cause he told me Etta would be there.'

'Well, that's where he said he was goin'. He even passed on a drink to get there. You must've missed him.'

'It's possible,' Rube muttered, uncertainly. 'What were you talkin' about?' he asked, still wondering about Etta.

'You. An' I do believe old Louis was gettin' himself into a light lather, vergin' on protective, you might say.'

Both men were thoughtful for a moment, and before either of them said any more, Peeler Bose spoke up.

'The marshal should be tellin' you that you ain't got a noose around your neck any more,' he said, cheerfully.

Behind Bose, his brother Walt was standing with Dow Lineman. 'Looks like just about everybody's hit town tonight,' Lineman observed.

Rube didn't want to get too involved. He wanted away, to do what he had to do. But Walt Bose was thinking otherwise, held up his hand as a restraining gesture.

'Cassidy,' he said. 'I don't know who owes who the drinks, but we're all of us deservin' o' one. It'll be a cold night in hell before we catch sight o' them bleatin' sons o' bitches again.'

Rube gave the men a long, speculative look. 'I been fightin' that kind since I was little more'n a weaner,' he said. 'But I just been tellin' one o' the creek farmers, that they *ain't* gone. They'll *never* be gone. Not until—'

Rube was mid-sentence when Louis Hark slammed the batwings aside. The man was wide-eyed, and his face was ashen as he reeled towards the bar. 'She's gone,' he said. 'Etta. She's gone. They must have got to her. I said for you to call on her,' he said, turning

131

to Rube. 'Did you see 'em . . . her . . . anythin'?'

'Hold up a minute,' Rube said. 'I thought it was odd, her not being there. But I guessed she was . . . well, I don't know, somewhere. Are you sayin' the sheepmen have taken her? Taken her hostage?'

'Who . . . what else? The back door's been busted off its hinges.'

The cattlemen shuffled their feet uneasily, gave each other troubled looks.

'I seen that Tekker Poole back o' town earlier,' Lineman said. 'He was swingin' a bottle. I reckon they drink their own sheep-dip.'

Hark swallowed a whiskey that Walt had set in front of him. 'They musta brought in a spare horse. Etta's bay was still in the shed stall,' he said, and coughed.

Again, Rube got to thinking of Tekker Poole. The man who was keeping his wounds green, the man he'd set out to look for.

'With respect, Louis, you ain't worth a plugged nickel, if it's a ransom they're after,' Sewett suggested to Hark. It don't add up.'

'It ain't goddamn money they want,' Hark retorted.

'No, it's me,' Rube said. 'Poole knows my weakness.' Rube now knew that Poole and his men had been tagging him for some time out at Wild Bird. They'd seen him with Etta, probably seen them kiss. 'I've got to get back to the ranch. It's where they'll have taken Etta. Where they'll want to trade her for

132

Wild Bird,' he explained.

Hark looked at Rube and saw the frame of mind, thought he understood.

'If what you say's true, the minute you sign them documents, they'll kill you,' the marshal chipped in.

'Yeah, I already thought o' that. So, I won't sign anythin' over until she's safe. We got no choice, an' I'm goin' alone.'

Dow Lineman nodded gravely. 'Within minutes o' you completin' that deal, an' Miss Etta bein' safe, we'll kill every sheepman within a hundred miles o' here.'

Rube grinned. 'Couldn't ask for more. Now I got to see someone about a bullet,' he said, and walked from the bar.

'I want every available man roused. *An'* them that ain't. I want 'em armed an' saddled an' outside o' here, ready to ride, within an hour,' Lineman said.

Out on the sidewalk, Dub Sewett stood watching the men who rode through the pools of thin lamp-light, along the street. Six of them reined in and dismounted, took note of the aggressive excitement around them. One of them, a big, heavily built man, nodded at the marshal as he led the way up the steps and through the batwings of the saloon.

From the opposite direction, Peeler Bose drew in his horse as Sewett was about to follow the men inside.

'Who the hell are them fellers, Dub?' he called out.

'Don't recognize any of 'em. But if they ain't with us, they's agin us. An' if they're sheepmen, I'll kill 'em on the spot, so help me,' the marshal responded harshly.

The newcomers were gathered at the bar. Standing near, beginning to look haggard and bleary-eyed was Louis Hark. He was talking to Amis Kalf and several cowboys.

Sewett went back in to the saloon, resolutely advanced on the tough-looking men. 'All you got to do is tell me you ain't sheepmen . . . or hired in any way by 'em,' he challenged.

The big man waited until he'd ordered up whiskeys and beers for his men, then he turned and gave Sewett a calculating look. 'Just *thinkin'* that, is a real bad thing where we come from, Marshal,' he said with a trace of intimidation. 'I'm Ansel Tribune, an' this here's Shave Renson, the man who brought Rube Cassidy's herd down from Cedar Springs.'

'Tribune huh,' Sewett said. 'Well, I guess I heard o' you.'

'An' I heard that somewhere in your jurisdiction, Rube's got himself in a mess o' trouble.'

'That's about the half of it,' Hark intervened angrily. 'I'da said my daughter's life was worth a thought.'

'What do you mean?' Tribune asked. 'What's your daughter got to do with this?'

'Her name's Etta, an' they took her . . . those goddamn sheepmen. *She's* the ransom for Wild Bird.'

134

Tribune was thinking while he swallowed his beer. 'Rube's a loyal man,' he asserted. 'There must be somethin' between him an' your daughter . . . Etta.'

'Yeah, I reckon I seen it. Newspaper editors ain't sorted for gunfightin', otherwise. . . .' Hark gave up on his wishful threat, banged down another empty glass. 'Rube'll be halfway out there by now,' he said.

Tribune studied his whiskey chaser. If Rube Cassidy's goin' to take out these sheepmen, he won't be doin' it out there, believe me,' he assured Hark and Sewett. 'There's time for me an' my boys to take on grub. Then we'll ride for Wild Bird. I'm getting' me a real interest in this territory.'

'Rube's sure forked over a steamin' heap o' trouble this time,' Renson said.

'Yeah, ain't he just,' Tribune agreed. 'But we'll get out there soon enough. We know he's got fresh horses . . . even who bred 'em,' he added wryly.

Hark suddenly pulled himself together. 'Mr Tribune,' he said. 'There's somethin' else that concerns me. I got a feelin' it's got some bearin' . . . needs to be sorted pretty damn quick. If you can come to the newspaper office, I'll explain on the way.'

22

OUT OF SIGHT

Five minutes later, in the *Coolidge Broadcast* office, Hark singled out an envelope from the locked drawer of his desk. He glanced at the writing on the front, then handed it to Tribune.

'You bein' here's got me to thinkin',' he said. 'I got a gut feelin' you should be readin' this. Go ahead an' open it.'

Ansel Tribune stood under an overhead lamp. Near poker-faced, he read the paper twice over.

Below the date, Rube Cassidy had written: *In the event of my death, I leave the property know as Wild Bird to Ansel Menander Tribune from Cedar Springs. This includes any cattle and livestock. If, with any of that property, Mr Tribune decides to reward whoever kills the man or men that kill me, I really ain't bothered. Signed, Ruben C. Bird.*

'He weren't one for lawful jargon, but he sure got the meanin' clear,' Tribune said, handing over Rube's note for Hark to read. 'I guess he knew I'd be actin' on his behalf. Some sort of avengin' kin.'

Hark refolded the paper, placed it back inside the envelope. 'You know who these men are that Rube's gone after?' he asked.

'Oh yeah,' Tribune said. 'I been advised real good.'

'You ain't got many men,' Hark suggested.

'That handful o' men are a hell of a lot more'n *many*,' Tribune responded sharply. With that, he turned and walked from Hark's office. But not before seeing the dread and helplessness in the newspaperman's eyes. 'Your daughter's safe enough,' he assured him. 'It's Wild Bird they want. Sounds pretty certain they won't get it if she's harmed.'

Near to midnight, Greasy Quorrel and Clete Winder rode ahead of Tekker Poole and Etta Hark. They approached a north bank crossing of Ten Mile Creek, moved slowly now, after a fast run from Coolidge. Occasionally, Winder dropped back to get a close look at Etta who rode ungagged and unbound. She'd lapsed into what the sheepmen took to be a brooding, frightened silence, but under their watchful eyes, her mind was racing with thoughts of breaking away.

Quorrel walked his horse into the creek water. 'Clete, Tekker,' he called, indicated that the two men and Etta ride around him. Then he twisted around in the saddle and called to another group of men who were following close. 'Barrow, you ride on now. When you get there, keep to the open ground, and call for him to come out. Tell him what's been arranged . . . the deal an' the girl.'

A tight, hunched man with a slung bandolier drew his horse alongside Quorrel. 'Jus' suppose he ain't at home. Jus' suppose he's standin' off from the house, watchin'. From what I've heard, this Cassidy feller ain't no widgeon.'

'Well, he won't shoot you. It's too dark, an' you're the one who's to lead him back to the girl. But, if he ain't there, go into the house and light a lamp. That'll bring him in, if he is watchin'. I'll be coverin' you when you're back on the trail.'

The man named Barrow sniffed and looked doubtful, heel-kicked his horse through the shallow water. The buildings of Wild Bird were further to the east, squat and dark in the moonlight.

Quorrel nodded at the two other men, then galloped ahead to the sandy steeps at the base slope of Springfield Ridge. As he rode, he scanned the darkness ahead, until he saw the riders ahead of him.

Winder saw him, pointed out to beyond where they rode. It was where many years of shrub and weed growth covered the bleached, broken bones of the Lagger sheep.

'Yeah, I know the place,' Quorrel said tellingly.

The trail the riders were on, sided tight to the base

of the ridge. The ground was broken shale, left virtu-
ally no sign for anyone who might be on their tail.
Quorrel knew they'd be coming, and who it would
be, felt secure in his choice of bolt hole. 'You know
it, Tekker. Take 'em on,' he said. 'Get yourselves
nested. I'm goin' to meet up with Barrow an'
Cassidy.'

Poole reined his horse away. He was followed by
Winder who was now leading Etta's mount. A quarter
of a mile further on, roosting birds fluttered into the
night sky. They were disturbed from the topmost
branches of a live oak, a lone tree that many years
before had split a wall of the ridge. Behind the broad
trunk was a deep cleft in the sandstone, a fault with
room for Poole, Winder and Etta Hark and their
horses. It would keep them well hidden from the
trail. It was a place Quorrel had learned of from
Poole. He'd got it prepared as a secure place to hold
the girl. If necessary, it was easily defended.

On the south fork of the creek, at the edge of the
willow stand, Rube was sitting his roan. He was deep
in thought as Hans and Frau's barking carried on the
night air.

Charging down the house would be a wrong thing
to do. For the moment, Rube knew that Etta would
come to no harm. They needed her for the deal,
would take good care of their trade goods. But after,
her life would be in as much danger as his own. Rube
knew that like himself, her life was expendable. As a

witness, she was already a dangerous liability to the sheepmen. But, for as long as she was alive and kicking, Rube could dicker. They were both safe up until the moment he signed his name. It wasn't much of a game, but he had to play it right.

He dismounted, ground-hitched the roan, and stamped his feet to get circulation moving. With his eyes aching to see in the darkness, he looked again towards the house, cursed softly when he saw the swing of a lantern in the distance. The yellow light beckoned, but he wasn't falling for it. It wasn't from a window, because he'd shuttered them all, and a visiting neighbour wouldn't have moved them aside.

The nerve at the corner of Rube's eye flickered and he grinned unkindly. Someone had unwittingly let the dogs out of their shed, so they would have given anyone trying to enter his house a hard time. Their sounds were definitely moving around fast, in and around the outbuildings.

There'd be more than one man up there, Rube supposed. Especially if they wanted to make a certain grab for him. But he didn't know, and that chewed away at his rising anger, his restraint.

There'd been no barking for a few minutes, and Rube decided it was time he made a move. Keeping low, he went forward, hoped Hans and Frau's attention would be diverted, that they'd sense *he* was out there.

They did, and when he was halfway to the house, they were on him. 'Hey, take it easy,' he said, as from

ten feet or more, both dogs went for him, chest high.
'Keep quiet for Chris'sakes. You'll get us all killed.'

Hans whined his displeasure at not being able to
go with the excitement, but both dogs obeyed him.
'Lie down,' Rube said. 'I won't be long. Just stay.'

Wide-circling the corral and his stock horses, Rube
neared the barn. From the cover of a stack of sawn
timber, he could see the front and side of the house.
He stood unmoving in the silence, couldn't hear a
thing, not even the sounds of any tethered saddle
horses. But they were on his land, he knew it, could
almost taste them being there. Then he realized that
they could be in the house, managed to get in when
the dogs had run off. Maybe they were on his bed
resting up, waiting for him, even now.

He pulled his Colt and walked determinedly to the
narrow rear door. Who the hell's goin' to feed all
these goddamn dogs, if I get a bullet? Rube was
worrying for the sake of it, while he listened again.
He tried the doorhandle, recalled it was a freshly-
greased movement. He let the door slide inward,
away from him. The' scullery was empty, but he could
smell the fresh bite of lamp oil as he stepped in. But
they couldn't be in any room of the house. If they
didn't know he was there, why should they be so
quiet?

He stepped into his bedroom, immediately felt the
coolness of the night, saw the lower half of his
window had been raised and left open. 'They've
been an' gone,' he said out loud. 'Now, they'll come

back, an' I'll be pinscher meat.'

Swearing, Rube ran back through the house, rushed headlong past the barn and the dog shed, where he guessed the pups were still fast asleep. Towards the creek, Hans and Frau were up and making swerving runs, excited again as they all ran for the ground-hitched roan. It was only then that Rube heard the sound of the riders. He went to ground, pulled the dogs in around him. He lay on his back, stared up at the sky. He wanted to listen and get a feel for his predicament, not allow it to overwhelm him.

In the flat, grey darkness before dawn, Rube rolled over to see the bunch of riders milling around the house and yard. A voice he recognized, rose above the general clamour.

'Rube. Rube Cassidy. You in there?' Peeler Bose called out.

'He ain't nowhere around. Let's ride,' an impatient voice shouted back.

Rube let out a long-held breath. It wasn't the sheepmen or their gunnies returning for him; it was the cowboys hoping for something to break. He should have known they weren't going to leave him as the lone battler. Etta's abduction was the trigger for their assault. And across the valley, others too, would be more than considerate. Of that, he was now sure. However, their presence did complicate the situation. They'd make any deal tricky, might even thwart it.

Rube watched while the men dismounted, saw them turn their horses into the corral. Then he had a long look around him, decided to make a run for the creekside willow and his roan. 'Now you can go!' he ordered the dogs, and pointed to the ranch house. 'That's where your food and hungry pups are. Go!'

23

WELL HIDEN

Rube rode west to Springfield Ridge. He knew the sheepmen would pull back when they discovered the rumpus they'd created. He gave them that much sense. But it meant he couldn't handle a fast transaction for Etta, wherever she was. There weren't many places to hide out in, only the ridge and its old trails and hidey-places that Rube had known from years back.

A half-hour later, he turned south along the shale, moved cautiously on from where the overgrown track led to the high, pine-topped rim. Keeping his eye on the broken walls of the ridge, he stayed east of the sandy steeps and the sheep bones. He was in little doubt that he was close to where his quarry was staked out.

Rube unsaddled the roan, and removed its bridle.

'Go home,' he said, and pulled his Winchester from its scabbard, slapped the horse's rump. 'Tell everyone, I may be a tad late.'

Watching his footfalls, careful not to send too much shale sliding down to the track below, Rube climbed fifty feet diagonally, up to an outcrop. With his back against the wall, he hunkered down on the spur. He laid the rifle beside him, pulled at the brim of his hat and waited quietly.

There was no sound, only the slightest of movements below him. Rube squinted, saw the dark, shiny flash of a coachwhip snake as it slithered through the rough track. Something or somebody had disturbed it from its home in the lone oak. It was what Rube knew to be the only timber along the old track. 'That's it,' he muttered. 'Behind the oak. If they're here, they're there. Poole knew about the fault.'

He knew there was no other way into the gap. He couldn't drop in unexpectedly from above, would have to take a chance and go around the oak.

Swearing with frustration, Rube inched his way back down to the trail. He was concerned that if he was caught there in the open, he'd be the turkey shoot. Then he sighted the branches of the tree, spreading high and wide across the ridge trail and the sandy steeps.

As he got closer, he realized that now *he* carried the advantage. He would see them at the same time as they saw him. But he was ready for it. With his eyes focused on the broad bole of the oak, he levelled the barrel of the Winchester.

Without warning, the jays squawked their way up from the branches again, and Rube flinched into a frozen silence. He knew a good lookout would have taken note of that disturbance, so he did their thinking. Instead of impulsively shrinking back, he went forward. Inch by inch, he eased the rifle around the oak trunk, worked his way through the gap until he could see the floor of the sandstone cleft ahead of him.

There was no sudden confrontation, and less than thirty feet away he saw Etta. She had a blanket draped around her shoulders, her back against the hump of a massive tree root. As far as he could tell, she was unharmed, not restrained in any way.

Clete Winder and Tekker Poole were standing beneath the angled overhang of a ridge wall. It sounded to Rube as though they'd been having a disagreement, was probably why they hadn't noticed the flight of the jays.

'We shoulda been out o' here before this,' Poole complained. 'Soon after sun-up, Greasy said.'

'There's been a hitch, maybe. What's a few hours?' Winder's voice was gruff and edgy.

'Hitches is what get men beefed.' The sound of creeping unease was evident in Poole's voice.

'Just can it, Tekker. We're safe enough,' Winder went on. 'They'll be here.'

'Yeah, if they ain't dead already. I told you fellers, the folk around here ain't goin' to overlook the kidnappin' of a newspaperman's daughter.'

146

'What is it you're really gettin' scared of?' Winder asked, with a low laugh.

'It's more of a bad feelin' than scared. You know what they say about best laid plans,' Poole said. 'There's history back of all this. I heard the old Lagger boss was lucky to escape with his life.'

'But escape he did,' Winder snorted. 'Now shut up whingeing. We're as safe as cubs here.'

Poole looked towards Etta. 'An' you reckon Cassidy's goin' to hand Wild Bird over in return for the kid?'

'Yeah, sure,' Winder said, and lowered his voice. 'Even love-struck enough to get himself killed doin' it, of Greasy says.'

'You got to remember she's goin' to be a leadin' witness in court. What's to prevent her puttin' us all behind bars?'

There was a few ominous moments of silence before Winder's response. 'What witness, what court?'

At that, Rube levered the rifle's trigger guard and stepped into the open. 'She won't be swearin' nothin' nowhere,' he said harshly. 'She won't have to: you two'll be long dead.'

'Rube Cassidy. It had to be him,' Poole snarled, groaned at his foreboding.

Wildly dragging at their holsters, Winder and Poole twisted to face Rube. But Tekker Poole didn't get to fire a shot. He managed to raise his gun hand, but that was all.

'Gotcha,' Rube rasped, as he fired a bullet into the man's belly. 'How's that for a real bad feelin'?' he added, and fired again as Poole's body hit the ground.

Winder's shots were missing, exploding against the bole of the oak. 'Where's Barrow?' he gasped. 'Where the hell's Quorrel?'

'They'll be here. At least you got *that* right,' Rube said, and fired point blank as Winder strutted forward, his face dark and thunderous with rage. Rube took a step back, thought of Etta who still hadn't made a move. But it was too late to look like a man who was shooting for gallantry. She'd seen the demonstration of Rube's long-held anger. Too bad, he thought in an instant, and levered the trigger guard, pulled the trigger again as Winder fell almost at his feet. That was it. Ten seconds of madly reverberating noise, a shadow of cordite smoke, and it was over.

'I wonder how your pa woulda writ that up?' he said dismissively, as he saw Etta moving towards him.

Before she could answer, he let the rifle fall to the ground and he put his arms around her, held her tight.

'How did you know that we were here . . . that *I* was here?' she asked after a long time.

'I didn't. But I knew there wasn't much any place else.'

Poole made a small grunting sound and tried to raise himself. But could only roll his head as Rube kneeled to listen.

'How *did* you find this place?' he said, breathless from a cold, waxy face.

'Saw a snake leavin'. Only meant one thing.'

'Quorrel never got to you then?'

Rube shook his head. 'No, he never did. I think he mighta tried though,' he said and stood back up. 'You couldn't leave alone could you, Poole? I guess you had to die here. Seems fittin' . . . for my family an' all.'

Poole shuddered. 'This sure is a cursed place,' he sputtered, and died, turning his face back to the dirt.

24

FAMILY SETTLEMENT

Three unsettled horses huddled close and trembled at the end of the fault. Rube nodded towards them. 'Let's see about gettin' you out o' here, before the place fills up,' he said.

'I'll ride with you to where the creek bends west. You ride for the ranch from there. The place is crawlin' with friendly guns, so you'll be good an' safe,' Rube said, as they tightened the cinches of a horse apiece.

'And you?' Etta asked, with near-to-tears sentiment.

'I'll come back. See if Poole's got any more to say.'

'Rubbish, he's dead. You're waiting for Greasy Quorrel. You think he's coming here. If he does, will you kill him, too?'

'That's a long question, Etta. But it's generally what I had in mind, yeah. Quorrel will just about complete my war budget. He'll certainly be the only one to begrudge it.'

'I'm not going back then. I'll stay to the end,' Etta asserted.

Rube rolled his eyes. 'Look, lady, I'm a real tough, blood-spittin' son-of-a bitch. So if you don't do as I say, I'll send you out o' here, pack-hitched to that snorter.'

'Why don't you tell me what it is you're saying then.'

Rube walked over to Poole's body, took the Colt from his outstretched fingers. 'Here, take this,' he said, handing it to Etta. 'It ain't been hardly used. Now, get yourself back under that blanket, an' stay there. I'm goin' to keep an eye on the track around this little hidey-hole. I need some warnin' of Quorrel getting' here, an' I'm guessin' he won't be alone.'

'I'm wantin' nothin' more'n a long ticket out o' this place,' Barrow rasped, as he and Quorrel drew their horses up to the big oak.

Rube was standing in the sandstone cleft, deep in the shadow of the oak. He listened, while the men sat their horses and talked.

'Now you can tell me where the hell it is you been?' Quorrel demanded. To Rube, it sounded like a question Quorrel had been asking since he'd met up with Barrow. 'Where the hell's Cassidy?'

'He never showed . . . not at the house,' Barrow retorted. 'I told you he wouldn't be easy meat.'

'What happened then? He musta been out there somewhere,' Quorrel said, in disbelief.

Rube breathed shallowly, listened to the men's exchange, Barrow's explanation.

'He was out there all right. I swung the lamp around to get his attention . . . if he was watchin'. Some goddamn, half-wild dogs got loose from a shed. Dogs you never told me about.'

Rube sucked a mouthful of air through his teeth, suppressed a wicked snigger.

'I got in to the house,' Barrow went on. 'Lucky there was no one there, so I waited. Then the dogs ran off, an' I wasn't goin' to hang around and find out why. Just as well, 'cause that's when a bunch o' cowboys rode in.'

'So Cassidy *was* in town,' Quorrel said. 'Takin' the girl's raised the stakes high. Still we're all safe enough here. I'll think on it for a while.'

'Well, I'm movin' on,' Barrow said decisively. 'Odds o' the ranchers, the settlers an' the law to one, ain't good. So, *no good*, I ain't even goin' to draw pay.'

Waiting for Quorrel's gunshot that never came, Rube backtracked quietly. He looked around, saw that Etta was curled up on the other side of the big root. He positioned himself to one side of her unmoving figure, wanted her well covered.

Quorrel whistled an impatient signal of his arrival as he pushed his way boldly into the fault. He was burning with the anger of Barrow's pulling out.

He saw a man standing in front of him, wasn't of an immediate frame of mind to look closely. 'How'd you make out here, an' where's the girl?' he started. Then he jerked on the reins, froze in his tracks.

The man before him wasn't Winder or Poole. It was the spectre of death, known as Rube Cassidy. Quorrel tried to swallow, but his throat constricted as he saw the bodies of Poole and Winder. There was no need for words of introduction. Quorrel knew that it was Rube who'd killed them.

Then the cunning, the instinct for survival overcame the grip of fear, and Quorrel went for the delaying tactic of a resigned smile. At the same time, he let himself fall sideways from the saddle. The first bullet from Rube's Winchester ripped past the side of his head, but as he hit the ground he plainly heard his own last rites.

'Make your peace, Quorrel,' Rube was saying as he fired a second time.

With a .45 bullet hammered into the top of one leg, Quorrel yelled, thrust himself up and forward on the other. He reached for the blanketed figure of

Etta, clawed desperately for his Colt as he landed.

Etta screamed, then her own Colt boomed, the sound muffled by the heavy blanket and the closeness of Quorrel's body.

The sheepman's body jerked back into the air, where it collected another round from Rube's gun. Quorrel saw Etta, then Rube advancing as his face smashed solidly into the hard wood of the oak root. Pulling the trigger was his last move, and he didn't feel the pain as the bullet from his gun drove deep into his belly.

'I told the law I'd be puttin' bullets in you one day,' Rube said, in a near whisper. Then there was the flicker of a smile, when he thought of telling folk that the sheep problem was over.

Etta kicked away the blanket, as Rube reloaded. She got to her feet and stared fixedly at him, didn't let her gaze stray to the dead men.

'Can we go now?' she asked.

'It was you, wanted to stay, remember?'

'Yes. And now I want to go. Before the horses die of fright.' Etta tugged at Rube's arm, handed him Poole's Colt.

'Are you sure Poole was one of them from when you were here before?' she asked, in a quiet voice.

They were sitting their horses at the south fork of Ten Mile Creek. Rube was holding the reins of the spare mount, a sturdy mare that had been stolen by the sheepmen from Ase Perry's farm.

154

'He was one o' their kind. Of *that*, I'm sure,' he answered brusquely. 'Now let's get to Wild Bird. Perhaps this time I can show you round proper.'

25

HOME TRUTH

The day was closing fast as Rube and Etta rode towards the home pasture of Wild Bird. In the yard, men and horses were milling around the glow of a camp-fire that brightened the dusk.

From the house, yellow lamplight glowed from a window and the open front door.

'Looks like a popular place to be,' Rube said drily.

'Sure does,' Etta agreed. 'Let's just hope the natives are friendly.'

Rube gave a whistle and shouted, laughed at the outbreak of frenetic barking.

Since the two of them had emerged from the creekside timber, a group of men had been watching their approach. Now, Dow Lineman and some cowboys moved apart, set for trouble. Then one of them let out a whoop and hurried forward.

'Hey Cassidy, is that you? Is that Miss Etta?' the Red-Iron man hollered.

Rube and Etta laughed. 'Yeah, it's us,' Rube shouted back. 'No need to search any more.' He raised a hand in greeting to Lineman. 'We'd be obliged if you'd send a rider to Coolidge . . . get word to Etta's pa,' he said. 'An' ask the marshal if he can send a burial detail out. The buzzards'll lead 'em to the spot.'

'Hey Ruben! Have you come back to thwart my new-found inheritance?' a voice boomed out cheerfully.

Rube turned from the cowboys to see Ansel Tribune standing in the doorway of his house. 'Hey, to you!' he returned. 'What the Sam Hill you doin' here?'

'Shave mentioned you was in some trouble.' Tribune took off his hat, nodded and smiled his introduction to Etta. 'We got hold of a bunch o' wool-asses. Missed the big horns though.'

Rube let go the reins of the mare, swung down from the saddle. 'That's 'cause I been takin' care of 'em. There should be more in a man's life than doin' domestic chores, don't you think?'

'Not entirely,' Tribune said. 'An' nor will you from now on, I'm thinkin'.'

'Uh huh,' Rube coughed, the inference not escaping him. 'So, where are you mutts?' he shouted.

Etta walked her horse alongside Rube. 'I'm spending more time here than I am in town,' she said. 'It's all right, but I do need to get back though. I'm going to ask Pa if *I* can write this story.'

'Is that why you asked about Tekker Poole?' Rube asked.

'Yes. Pa says the truth's everything. And that's why there's never enough column space for it. It's his benchmark joke.'

Rube smiled broadly as he kneeled to fondle his pinschers. 'I'll ride in with you. There's somethin' I got to ask him too,' he said, 'but it'll wait until tomorrow.' Then he yelped as the pups nipped his fingers.